Bluebird Sky

EMI HILTON

Darrell & Page

For my three children, Ethan, Evan and Connor

Chapter One

Emma flew down the mountain as her skis slid through the powder packed snow. The crisp winter air whipped her hair, making it fluttery and loose. Today, she was young and care-free. The debacle of the last week, a distant memory. Stretching her neck, she let the sunlight bathe her in its rays. The perfect bluebird sky engulfed her in its beauty, dissipating her heartache. The wide-open space, with its miles of endless shimmery snow, wiped her soul clean.

Glancing over her shoulder, Emma located her mom. Melanie trailed behind her at a slower and more manageable pace. Bringing her eyes back to the slope of the run, Emma glided perfectly around the bumpy path. Breathing in the pine filled air, she sighed with delight as the reminders of winter danced around her nostrils. Her racing thoughts silenced, and she basked in the tranquility.

"Emma. Slow down!" bellowed Melanie. The sound carried all the way down the mountain, and her ears picked up her plea.

Usually, she skied at the same pace as Melanie, but not

today. She had nothing to lose. Emma squinted over her shoulder once more, locating Melanie, still several yards away. Turning back around, she faced the upcoming curve of the mountain. "Don't worry about me! It's a bluebird sky in Bluebird!" Emma squawked back. "It doesn't get much better than this!"

Effortlessly, she skied through the moguls, gleefully laughing at each rise and fall. With every twist and turn of the course, her confidence went up a notch. After a year's absence from the sport, she had managed to maintain her skiing skills.

"Emma!" repeated Melanie. Her name dangled in the air.

Annoyed by her mom's insistence, she rolled her eyes. "I'm fine!"

The sound of her skis gliding over the slope rang in her ears. She grinned, exhilarated by her speed. Then, with only a split second to react, she shrieked.

Her stomach plummeted, while her heart ground to a halt.

A few feet in front of her was a huge, jagged rock. With no time to adjust the direction of her skis, she hit it. Hard. For three glorious seconds, she coasted freely through the air. Light as a feather and free as a bird, she reveled in the sensational feeling of flying. Her mind quickly catalogued every major moment of her life like an overly fast slideshow. As the last image lingered, she questioned everything. *This might be the end. This could be it.* Perhaps it was her destiny to meet her extinction, as a newly single, soon to be spinster.

Heartbeat pulsating in her temples, her voice cracked, "I don't want to die!"

Instantly, her cry was swallowed up in the grand open space, like every sound in the universe had been eerily silenced.

Time had no meaning, while the seconds, which seemed like an eternity, ticked by, she neared a bone-crushing stop. With no idea how to save herself, Emma lunged her head backward as hard as possible to keep herself from slamming face first into the tree in front of her. The knee jerk reaction helped. She skidded to a stop, a mere inch from colliding into it.

Heart exploding, she gasped for breath. Ears ringing, she croaked, "I'm fine."

The words a lie. A weak attempt to control the uncontrollable. Over the past week, her world had been rocked in more ways than one. If she had learned anything, Emma knew she wasn't in control. The truth was, nobody was.

With snow piled up to her neck, she couldn't move a single solitary muscle. Her vision blurred. With no where to look but up, she glanced toward the brilliant crystal-clear blue sky. A bad, bad choice. The blinding sunlight overhead sent shock waves through her brain, causing her temples to throb. She swore she saw stars.

This is the end.

Slamming her eyes shut, she took deep cleansing breaths like she was sitting in the front row of her yoga class. This couldn't be her fate. Or was it? To die alone?

An unfamiliar voice pierced through her psyche. "Wake up." The words sounded distant. The annoying shout continued. The words were much louder and no longer fuzzy.

She fluttered her eyes open just a tad, but the glaring light of the sun made concentrating difficult. Blinking rapidly, she fought to stay awake. "Yes." She managed with one eye popped open.

Unable to recall anything other than the sensation of flying, she attempted to move. It was useless. Snow packed her in tighter than sardines in the little tin can.

Someone moved in front of her vision, perfectly blocking out the bright sun. The relief was immediate. Her head cleared enough for her to concentrate on his face.

"Can you hear me?" A man with a chiseled jawline and dark wind-swept hair crouched in front of her. Ski goggles covered his eyes, but she was positive if he removed them, a set of dazzling blue eyes would peek out from under them.

"Yes," she croaked. "I can hear you." Emma forced herself to stare at his goggle-covered face to avoid double vision. She studied the weeks' worth of stubble he had undoubtedly trimmed to perfection.

Where was her mom? How long had she been there? Was she paralyzed? The questions came in rapid succession, causing anxiety to bubble up her chest.

The man turned to an unknown figure to her right, one she couldn't see. "She's awake. Don't move her. We don't know if she's damaged her spine, neck, whatever. We need to wait for the ski patrol to get here." He spoke with confidence, like a man used to taking charge.

"Mom?" she sputtered.

"I'm here, honey." Melanie's voice came from outside of her line of vision. "Don't worry... I'm sure they'll get you out real soon." The words were slow, each one calculated like she was attempting to tamper her anxiety.

"I can't see you. Where are you? I can't move." Emma's pulse raced. Bile burned its way up her throat, leaving a trail of acid. Head spinning, vision doubled, she found it hard to continue the conversation.

"Don't worry... I can't get any closer, but I can see you." A long arduous pause followed. "We're going to get you help," replied Melanie.

Her heart picked up to a staccato beat. Sheer unrestrained panic pumped through her veins with each thump. Skiing like she had a death wish. Best care scenario, she came out of this whole ordeal with a few broken bones. That was the *best* case. Reality struck. She wasn't dead, but she might have permanently injured herself.

"Don't move," said the hot former model.

His words snapped her out of her daze. She cleared her throat, studying the curves of his face. "I can't move, even if I wanted. I'm completely stuck."

The man turned, peering over his shoulder. While he glanced away, Emma checked out his flawless silhouette. A face the Greek sculptors would have chiseled into stone. He turned back to stare at her. Then he pulled up his ski goggles, resting them on his forehead. Piercing baby blues stared back at her. She called it. His eyes were the color of ocean waves. Not murky Pacific Ocean waters, but Mediterranean Sea blue. She must have died, and this was heaven.

"I mean it." His gaze moved across her face.

"Okay." She gulped. "I won't."

She willed herself to focus on him, but her vision became black and blurred once more. With no choice, she slammed her eyes shut to keep the world around her from becoming topsy-turvy. It was imperative she made the pulsating pain in her temples lessen. Emma dared to hope that when she opened her eyes again, her vision would be restored. Even more, she dared to dream that the man with dazzling eyes would still be there.

A part of her heard those around her talking. The voices were too far distant for her to make them out clearly. The guy with the piercing baby blues dipped and dived through her subconsciousness. She wondered who he went home to at night. Was she beautiful? Talented? Whomever this imaginary woman happened to be, Emma hoped she appreciated the magnificent gift he was to women. All women. His rugged good looks were worthy of making any woman swoon.

The piercing sound of the snowmobile grinding across the icy slope made her whip her eyes open. From her blocked view, she made out the ski patrol on a snowmobile barreling toward her.

"She's awake again!" Melanie squealed from out of her field of vision. "That's a good sign, right?"

She concentrated on staying awake like it was her sole purpose in life.

"Too soon to tell," said the man who had come to her rescue. "What's your daughter's name?"

The voices surrounded her as commotion rippled out. A crowd must have gathered with all the chatter she heard but couldn't see.

"Emma," stated Melanie.

The man came back into view, crouching down next to her once more. His voice was steady and calm as he said her name.

"The ski patrol is here. They're going to dig you out and get you to help."

"Fine." Her stomach churned. She swallowed down the bile creeping up her throat, making the acid burn all the way to her stomach.

Two ski patrols began digging around her with shovels. The tight grip of the densely packed snow slowly loosened with each scoop. Slight feeling returned to her body, and soon her limbs were restored some mild movement.

"I can still move my arms!"

"Hallelujah," exclaimed Melanie.

After a few more minutes of digging, Emma's shoulders and arms became free. She shot them out in front of her like a cannon. With some mobility restored to her head and neck, she took in the whole slew of people gathered around her. Embarrassed, heat splashed her cheeks.

"Nothing to see here." Emma attempted to wave off the crowd. "I'm going to be fine... just fine. Please go back to skiing."

Mortified, she kept her head down, avoiding eye contact with all those who had stopped to stare. The ski patrol continued to dig and soon her legs were freed. Once loose, she crawled out of the pit and onto the harder flat packed snow of the ski run.

"Whoa, there... Where do you think you are going?" One of the snow patrols grabbed her firmly, forcing her flat against the stretcher hooked to the back of the snowmobile.

"Please stop! This isn't necessary." Searching the crowd, Emma struggled to find her mom, and the ski patrol tightened the straps around her shoulders. "I don't need to be carried down the mountain!"

Melanie popped up out of the crowd.

"Emma, they know what they're doing." Melanie reached out, squeezing her hand. "Don't fight them. Please, let them do their job."

Emma scanned her face, spotting deep worry lines growing around her eyes. *This was bad. Real bad.*

The ski patrol finished tightening the straps around her ankles.

"I'm *so* embarrassed." Frustrated that nobody was listening to her, Emma attempted to wiggle free.

Rescue man knelt on the side of the stretcher opposite from her mom. Leaning over her head, he blocked her view of the bluebird sky. All she saw was him. Him, and his dazzling set of baby blues. Her heart fluttered while molten lava pumped through her veins. She smelled his minty breath, along with his tangy aftershave. She willed herself to focus and not let her mind wander down a fantasy path of what would never be.

"I agree with your mom. Let them do their job." His voice was smooth. He broke their physical barrier, touching her lightly on her arm. Though she had on layers of clothing, she swore her arm warmed from his fingertips. "It'll be a lot easier... promise."

Emma gulped. She tried to speak, but couldn't. Her mind

refused to work. Maybe it was the fall? Perhaps. Most likely, it wasn't that at all. No, it was the man with his hand on her arm, making her skin tingle.

Melanie interrupted her scattered, incoherent words. "Emma. Enough." Her voice was laced with irritation, commanding her to listen.

Strapped in tight, Emma had no choice. Her vision became blurry again. The adrenaline coursing through her body dissipated. She began to feel woozy and disoriented.

"Okay," mustered Emma. Her heavy eyelids closed, blocking the view of her mom, and the man with the gemstone eyes.

The ride down the mountain was smooth and cathartic, so she drifted off to sleep until some jostling woke her. The medics lined up her stretcher's wheels to the back of the ramp of the ambulance. She flicked open her eyes.

Confused, Emma asked, "Where am I?"

The open bluebird sky filled her vision, miraculous in splendor and annoyingly perfect. She attempted to move, but it was fruitless. The straps bound her. Every part of her body ached, and her skin stung with pain.

"Bluebird Mountain," stated the now familiar voice of the local hero.

"Bluebird Mountain." Emma repeated.

That's right. She was on a ski trip with her mom, Melanie. The ski trip which was supposed to be her honeymoon. The one she had meticulously planned to be during her winter break from teaching elementary school.

Only last week, at their rehearsal dinner, her fiancé, Jake, had called off their wedding. Jake told her he didn't love her. Not anymore, and while he was being honest, he never really had. Emma didn't know what was worse. The humiliation of calling off a wedding during a rehearsal dinner or the realization that the last two years of her life had been a complete lie. Jake had made *her* the place holder. The woman he stayed with but was willing to ditch if his number one decided to come along. Best part, he had zero remorse. He was cold and distant while resolved in his choice. He was a far cry from the man with whom she had once fallen in love.

So, when he stood outside the restaurant and confessed he couldn't marry her, Emma wanted to die.

Die.

Like take me now, I have nothing to live for.

Like this can't be my life.

Like this can't be happening.

Only it was happening. And it was her life.

Unlike Jake, who stated he had never loved her; she had unapologetically loved him. Emma thought her wildest dreams were coming true. Then, whoosh, one fell swoop took it all away.

Who did he love? She questioned him, demanding to know the truth. The man was leaving her high and dry. The truth was the one thing he owed her. With how well she knew Jake, a man who hated being alone more than anything in this world, there was someone else. Then again, wasn't there always?

A girl from high school, he confessed. The words left his mouth effortlessly, like he had nothing to hide. Like it was a Sunday morning, and the two of them were discussing brunch options. Because it was only her world shattering, and not his.

The old flame had drifted back into Jake's life the month prior, at a chance meeting in the grocery store. She was newly divorced, and when he saw her again after all these years, he realized he loved her, always had. He realized he hadn't ever loved Emma. Not really. Not at all. Not like he loved this girlfriend of the past. So, he was taking his chance. Surely, he thought, Emma wouldn't fault him for following his heart. But what about Emma's?

All these events swiftly landed her on her honeymoon with her *mother*. Skiing ruthlessly, she tried to forget. All. Of. It. Every little bit.

Somehow, she thought the skiing, the taking risks, would miraculously help her bypass some of the agony. Even for a minute.

It didn't work, obviously. She failed miserably.

Tears clouded her limited vision, flowing down the side of her temples. With no ability to wipe them away, they cascaded onto her shoulders, seeping into her sweater under her ski jacket, making a damp mess.

Melanie's voice snapped her back to the present, when she said, "Don't cry. It'll be okay."

"I'm trying." Emma spoke to the bluebird sky above her. If God was up there, now was the time for him to make his appearance. Listen to her plea for help. She was barely surviving.

"Don't cry. I hate it when I see a woman cry." He was back. The steady hero living up to his role. A man, though she knew nothing about, didn't seem anything like Jake.

Emma gritted her teeth as the name of her ex sneaked its way back into her psyche. It further incited her anger.

"I'll try to stop." She swallowed, shooting the fiery mention away.

"That's it," said the skiing hero hottie. "Calm down and don't worry. It'll all be okay."

If only.

More than anything, she wanted to see his face one last time. A memory of him for the road. One she could dream about when the nights in her future were sure to be spent alone, but all she saw was the irritatingly exquisite bluebird sky. Scratch and scrap went the wheels of the stretcher. Recoiling from the sound, she locked her jaw as the medics pushed her stretcher up the ramp into the back of the ambulance. The medic leaned out the back to shut the door.

View completely obstructed, Emma called out the ambulance door. "Wait! What's your name?"

"Sean," he replied.

Sean. The doors of the ambulance slammed shut. She flinched. The bang vibrated back and forth, causing her ears to ring. The world around her spun off its axis.

Beeping filled the cramped space of the ambulance. She was hooked up to a myriad of machines. The medics poked and prodded, but she felt nothing. Her being numb. A series of questions followed. Being a good patient, she tried her best to answer while weird drifting memories wandered through her mind, but none of them were solid. Only one thing finally took hold of her, Sean and his dazzling blue eyes and dark wind-swept hair. The man who would never bail on a woman or promise someone the moon only to yank it back. Nah. He was different, one of the good ones. She felt it in her bones.

A grip tightened around her arm, placing it into a blood pressure sleeve. The medic spoke, but she didn't hear the words. When she didn't answer, the medic peered over her face.

She blinked, suddenly remembering how to speak. Emma asked, "What was that? I couldn't hear you."

"Can you feel your toes?" The medic bent over her, waiting for a reply.

Brain, concentrate. She cleared her raw throat. "Yes. I can feel them."

With her arm in the medic's hand, they responded, "Very good."

The no nonsense medic stabbed something into the big

vein on her right arm. The liquid seeped into her body, melting away the aching pain like the snow in the spring. Gone, she was wiped clean. The medicine pulsed through every fiber of her being, while she wished to be made whole.

The struggle to stay awake real. Emma closed her eyes and welcomed the darkness to overtake her. And it did.

Chapter Two

"Do you know where they are taking her?" asked Melanie.

Sean and Melanie watched the ambulance drive away from the parking lot of the ski lodge. What a strange day? He certainly hadn't anticipated any of this happening when he woke. Living right next to the mountain, he spent any few moments he had, during the winter, on the slopes. This morning, it was a last-minute decision to go skiing before his afternoon appointments. Perhaps his own brush with destiny.

He forced himself back to the conversation. "Yes. This is a small town, and there's only one hospital."

Once the ambulance turned onto the road and out of view, he brought his gaze back to Melanie. The two of them had chatted and introduced themselves to each other while the ski patrol dug Emma out of the tree well.

Relief washed over Melanie's face. "Really? Would you mind writing down the address for me? We're here on vacation, and I don't know where anything is located." Eyes wide, she peered back at him eagerly. "I certainly didn't think I'd need to know the location of the nearest hospital." She threw her hands down at her side.

Sean, a bit of a people-pleaser, had done his duty and made sure Emma got into the ambulance. Nobody would fault him if he went back into the ski lodge to eat a snack and hit the slopes again. But there was something about Emma, an intangible connection, one which he couldn't describe. What was he even thinking? He didn't believe in any of that.

Nevertheless, when he told Melanie she could follow him to the hospital, he was shocked.

Melanie shifted on her feet, glancing down. "I can't let you do that. You've done enough already." She waved off the offer. "Just write down the address, and I'll look up the directions on my phone."

Sean adjusted his beanie, pulling it over his ears to block out the wind nipping at his skin. "Nonsense. I insist. I can't abandon you now." Sean dug his keys out of his pocket, fiddling with them, he continued. "I'm invested. I want to make sure you leave here knowing there are good people who live in Bluebird."

Melanie peered up from her feet and asked, "you promise you don't mind?"

Sean smiled. "I promise. It's no trouble at all." Glancing over his shoulder, he looked for his car. Once he spotted it, he reverted his attention back to Melanie. "Now, where are you parked?"

She pointed in the same direction as his car. They made their way across the parking lot. The morning sun had turned the icy concrete to a wet, slushy mess.

Sean settled into his car, cranking up the heat to make the windows defrost. Once Melanie pulled up behind him, he backed out and slowly made his way out of the parking lot. The roads were slippery. He kept his speed slow and steady to prevent his wheels from sliding. Every minute or so, he glanced in his rear-view mirror to ensure Melanie was still behind him as he drove across town.

On the drive, he tapped on the steering wheel to the beat of the music blaring from his radio. Here he was again, having to be the hero. Rushing in to the save the day, when Emma and Melanie were more than capable of handling the situation. Why did he feel heavily invested in making sure Emma was okay? People had access to maps at the touch of a fingertip, but no, he had insisted.

Emma. Her eyes had drawn him in at first sight. When she stared back at him with her brilliant hazel eyes, eyes which mirrored slick granite with its mix of colors, he found it hard to look away. Every part of him ached to protect her, to right every wrong. She was a damsel in distress, and he lived to help anything or one in need.

Women always sucked him in, then left him high and dry. As nice as Melanie and Emma appeared, he knew in the end they were probably like all the rest. The women in his life had reeled him in, taken him captive, then dumped him the minute someone or something better came along. And he fell for it every single time. Like a true sucker.

His mom was a perfect example. One day when he was eleven, he came home from school and found his dad sitting on the couch looking blankly out the window. All he explained was his mom had left and wasn't coming back. No warning. Nothing. Snap, gone.

For years, he waited and hoped for her return, thinking she would one day wake up and realize how much she missed him. Being a child, he blamed himself. If he had only been better, smarter, less of a bother and more of a help, then perhaps she would return. She never did. His mom walked away and never looked back. No calls, cards, or gifts. Nothing. A clean break for her. Sean never recovered. Today, all these years later, he carried the scars of his past like a child's comfort blanket.

Through the years since his mom left, he reminded himself at every turn to never let a woman get too close. If he did, they might not like what they see. His mom didn't. The few times he opened his world, he regretted it. Afterwards, he remembered the pain that came when you let someone in, and they left. Instead, he built a steel trap around his fragile heart, keeping everyone at an arm's length. Whenever he suspected an ounce of disinterest, he booked it to the nearest exit. With his life in his own control, he promised himself nobody was ever leaving him again. He would do the leaving.

Then today, without even looking for it, Emma drew him in the moment he spotted her getting off the ski lift at the top of the mountain. The very air in his lungs was knocked out of his chest. Gracefully gliding down the mountain at a speed he had never seen, he had trailed behind her out of curiosity. The way she had shifted and turned with no care left him in awe. The woman was fearless. Then when she took a bump way too fast, he gasped, heart skidding to a halt. Her body drifted through the air like a plastic shopping bag floating with the wind. When she finally landed, he thought for sure she was dead.

Melanie was out of sorts when he skied over to see what help was needed. Even when the ski patrol came, he stayed with her, because the woman clearly loved and cared about Emma. A scene which thawed a smidge of his heart. Sean, who hadn't thought about his mom in years, was surprised by how much he still longed for a mother's love.

The hospital was only a few minutes away, and soon Sean pulled into the empty parking lot. Bluebird was a small town in Vermont, not a place of a lot of action. People had to drive to the nearby big cities if they desired more. Honestly, it was a blessing they even had a hospital. Most likely it was only there because of the ski slopes.

Melanie pulled into the spot next to him and got out. He joined her.

Clearing his throat, he shoved his keys into his pocket.

"The ER is right through there." He pointed to the entrance, clearly marked. Man, he was acting foolish. Obviously, the woman could read.

"I've got it. Thanks for your help." Melanie shifted her purse onto her shoulder, glancing toward the entrance. She swung her eyes back to him, smiling. "I truly appreciate it."

Sean mirrored her smile. "No problem. I'm happy to help." Melanie shuffled her feet, but before she left, he added, "if you get hungry, the hospital happens to have an excellent cafeteria."

Here he was babbling. This was his cue to leave. To drive away. Allow Melanie to check on Emma. Emma. Was she okay? His stomach plummeted. Heart clenched. His mind flashed to a hypothetical scene of Melanie crying all alone in the hospital.

Melanie nodded. "Thanks for the tip... good to know. Though I hope I won't be here long enough to find out." She forced a smile, her lips forming a crooked line. "Thanks again... you're truly our knight in shining amour."

Sean shrugged, but the words were music to his ears. "It wasn't a big deal. I did what anyone would do." He straightened his shoulders.

"No. Not true." Melanie sighed, eyes suddenly cloudy and dark. "I hope Emma can find a guy like you someday." Her jaw locked, she continued, "At least someone better than the jerk who left her the day before her wedding."

"What?" Sean took a step closer to her, intrigued by this piece of information. The woman was gorgeous. Who in their right mind would leave her?

Somber, Melanie nodded.

"The guy left her the day before their wedding?" asked Sean.

Melanie cleared her throat. "Yes. It's true. It's been a horrible two weeks." She tightened the grip on her purse.

17

"Anyway. I should get going. It was nice meeting you. Thanks again." She waved, then started toward the hospital entrance.

When she was halfway across the parking lot, Sean's legs moved without his consent. Jogging to catch up with her, he was clearly possessed. He needed to let the lady go. But. He. Couldn't. Something in him needed to know Emma had survived the whole ordeal. What if Melanie was about to receive horrible news? Alone. The thought made him shudder.

"Wait!" Sean caught up with her, falling into step next to her. Melanie glanced at him, blinking. Unsure if he was being a nuisance or help. He pressed forward and said, "let me come with you. I'll only wait with you until you know Emma is safe. If there happens to be bad news, I don't want you to be alone when you receive it."

Melanie gave a curt nod. "That's certainly thoughtful of you."

He exhaled. Maybe the lady didn't think he was pest after all? "I've lived here my whole life. Even broke a few bones as a child, so I've been here enough to know my way around the place."

Leading her into the hospital, he helped her locate the ER check in. The front desk had a nurse behind it, she was on the phone when they stopped in front of it. She held up a single finger for them to wait. Finally, she hung up. Glimpsing up, she asked, "how may I help you?" She shuffled some papers around on her desk.

"Hi. We're checking to see if Emma..." Sean turned, peering at Melanie. He didn't even know this woman's last name.

"Arden," added Melanie.

"Let's see." She stopped sorting. "Give me a minute to bring up the information. Are you family?" asked the nurse. She typed on her keyboard but stopped, eyeing the two of them.

Melanie nodded. "I'm her mother."

"Very well then." The nurse went back to typing on the keyboard.

Melanie gnawed at her fingernails. Clearly her carefree, nonchalant behavior from before was long gone, replaced by pent up nerves.

The nurse stopped typing. Her eyes landing on the two of them, she cleared her throat. "The information is right here." Pointing at to her computer screen, she continued, "Emma Arden was admitted here a few minutes ago. Brought in by ambulance... is that correct?"

Melanie leaned over the counter, peering at the nurse's computer screen. "Correct. Do you have any other update beside that?"

"She was in a ski accident at Bluebird Mountain. We're worried it could be serious," added Sean.

He leaned against the front desk, reverting his attention from the nurse to the swinging doors which led to triage. Somewhere behind those doors was Emma. He hoped she was okay.

The nurse shifted in her seat. "I don't have any other information, but I'll let the doctor treating her know you're waiting for an update." She pointed to the empty chairs which filled the waiting room, before she added, "please feel free to take a seat."

Melanie wrung her hands. "Okay... I guess that's what we'll do."

They both walked over to the empty chairs, settling into them. Neither said anything, but his stomach started to rumble. With a desire to be helpful, he rapidly stood.

Melanie flinched at his rapid movement. She fiddled with her purse straps on top of her lap.

He cleared his throat. "I'm going to grab something from

the cafeteria." Sean shoved his hands into his pockets. "You've got to be hungry. Can I get you anything?"

Melanie waved him off. "No. I'm fine. Thanks." Her voice barely above a whisper.

Sean rubbed the back of his neck. "I'll grab a few random things, then if you do decide you're hungry, you can eat it later."

Melanie blinked. "Okay..." Her voice trailed off.

Sean left her in the waiting room, wandering down to the cafeteria. From the snack bar, he grabbed a few different drinks and snacks. After paying, he engulfed a protein bar on his way back to the waiting room. Entering the room, he spotted one of his clients. He strode over to him.

"Dr. Liberman," Sean approached the check-in desk. Dr. Liberman glanced up from the clipboard he was writing on. "How's Daisy doing?"

A look of recognition crossed his face. Dr. Liberman smiled. "Doc, what are you doing here? Is everything okay?"

"Maybe you can help me? I came in with a woman who was injured skiing at Bluebird Mountain." Sean shifting his feet, peering over at Melanie, who was watching them closely. He gave her a slight wave and pointed in her direction. That's her mom over there waiting for an update. I don't suppose you could do me a favor and check on her?"

Dr. Liberman looked over Sean's shoulder at Melanie. Then returned his attention to Sean. "What's the name of the patient?"

"Emma Arden."

Dr. Liberman picked up his clipboard, shoving his pen into his lap coat pocket. "Sure." He pointed over his shoulder with his clipboard toward the swinging doors which led to the emergency room. "I'll go check and see if I can find out about an update."

Sean held his hand out to Dr. Liberman. "I'd really appreciate it. Thank you."

Dr. Liberman shook his hand with a small smile. "Anything for my favorite veterinarian."

"Only veterinarian in town, but I'll take the compliment," added Sean.

He laughed. "I'll be right back." Dr. Liberman turned, pushing open the swinging doors to triage.

Sean wandered back to where Melanie waited, sitting down next to her. Digging into his plastic bag, he held out a water bottle for her. She took it. Next, he held out a few snacks for her to choose. "Dr. Liberman is going to go and check on Emma. He'll see if he can give us any sort of update."

Melanie took the bag of pretzels. "Thanks." She fiddled with the bag before finally opening it. "That's certainly nice of him. How do you know him?"

"I treat Dr. Liberman's Yorkie," said Sean.

"Really?" Melanie slowly ate a pretzel before she asked, "you're a veterinarian?"

Sean nodded. "Yes, I'm. Only one in town. I took over the practice from my dad." He took a sip of water then rummaged through the snacks, deciding on the potato chips. "He was a vet for over thirty-five years and retired a few years ago. Now he spends his time golfing and traveling around in his RV visiting national parks." He opened the bag, popping a chip into his mouth.

"Fascinating." Melanie ate a few more of her pretzels in silence.

Both continued eating their respective snacks. A few minutes later, Dr. Liberman came through the swinging doors toward them with a medical chart in his hand. Melanie jumped up from her seat. Sean stood.

Melanie, with wide-eyes, voice laced with concern, asked, "Any update?"

Dr. Liberman scanned the chart in his hands. "Yes. Looks like her CT scan and MRI came back normal. No sign of paralysis. That's all very good news." He glanced up from the chart. "She most likely has a concussion. She'll have to stay overnight to be monitored. I'd say, overall, she's a lucky lady."

Melanie clapped her hands together, exhaling. "That's wonderful news. Thank you so much for the update."

"No problem. Any friend of Dr. Beckett is a friend of mine. I'm glad I could deliver some good news, which isn't always the case with my job." Dr. Liberman glanced at his watch. "I need to run, but the nurse will come to take you to her in a little while."

Melanie held her hand out. "Thanks again Doctor."

Dr. Liberman shook it. "My pleasure. See you later, Dr. Beckett."

Sean shoved his hands into his pockets. "Yes, see you soon."

Both settled back into their seats.

Melanie's shoulders dropped like a visible weight had been lifted from them. "I'm so relieved." She held her hand against her heart. "I didn't know how this all was going to turn out. I tried to act upbeat as not to alarm Emma, but man, she's one lucky lady. This could've ended badly."

Leaning back in his seat, Sean propped one ankle over his knee. "Emma is certainly fortunate. She might need to start buying lotto tickets." He paused. A long beat of silence filled the space between the two of them. Shifting in his chair, acutely aware he had overstayed his welcome. Emma was in the clear. Time for him to make his exit. He stood. "I'm glad Emma's fine. I think I'm going to head out. Are you okay to be alone while you wait to be led to her room?"

Melanie glanced up, nodding. "Yes, I'm good. I appreciate all your help today. You've gone above and beyond. It's nice to know there are still good people in the world like you."

Sean brushed off the compliment but returned it with a small smile. The words made him pull back his shoulders. He bent down, gathering up his trash. As a last thought, he opened his wallet and pulled out a business card. "Here's my business card." He held it out to her. "Please don't hesitate to call if you need any additional help while you're here in Bluebird."

Melanie took the business card, fiddling with it between her fingertips. She shook it. "Thanks again." Her lips formed a tight smile.

"Of course..." Sean's back straightened. "My pleasure."

Before he passed through the sliding glass doors, he peeked one last time at Melanie. She wasn't looking in his direction. Instead, she was studying his business card.

Continuing to the outside, the cold air hit his body, making him shiver. He jogged the rest of the way to his car, cranking up the heat after he settled into his seat. Patiently, he rubbed his hands together to keep them warm while he waited for his windows to defrost. What an odd day. The day certainly hadn't gone how he planned, but for whatever reason only getting one run down the slopes didn't bother him in the least. Helping a damsel in distress always boosted his ego. It didn't hurt this damsel was most beautiful woman he had ever met. The car finally warm, his mood light, he drove home.

Chapter Three

The blinding florescent lights above her hospital bed made Emma's temples throb. A steady amount of pulsating pressure beat against her skull. She closed her eyes again to mellow the pain. Shifting in her hospital bed, it creaked under her weight. Rising an arm, she slung it over her eyes. Every part of her ached. Groaning, she gritted her teeth to block out the waves of pain. Not only did she hurt physically, but emotionally, she was teetering close to a break down.

After a series of tests and scans, the doctors informed her she was lucky to come out of the whole ordeal with a simple concussion. Lucky? She balked at the idea. There was one thing she wasn't, and that was lucky. Though, she thoroughly admitted her reckless skiing had been a huge mistake. Being jilted the night before her wedding had highly impaired her judgement. Obviously, she needed to pull herself together. Who knew what type of shenanigans she might try next?

In a few days, she had to return from winter break and inform her students and co-workers that she wasn't married. No need to call her by a new name. The woman was single. *Single.* The word ricocheted back and forth in her mind. Last time, she was single was when she was dumped her senior year of high school after a lacrosse game. Tears ran rampant down her temples, cascading onto her pillow. Emma made zero attempt to stop it. Not today, she was leaning into the pain.

In the midst of her pity party, a voice broke her dark and awful thoughts. "Emma. I was so worried about you." Melanie's voice forced her eyes wide open. "Are you okay?"

Melanie crossed through the doorway and came over to her bedside.

Emma attempted to sit. "I know, Mom. Please don't remind me. The whole thing is a complete fiasco." She swiped at the fresh tears which clouded her vision.

The only bright spot in her terrible day was the cute guy, Sean. If she closed her eyes long enough, she could see him with his ski googles resting on his forehead. She wistfully sighed.

Melanie reached out, giving Emma's hand a quick squeeze while Emma reverted eye contact.

"The doctor said you have a concussion." Melanie made a tsk sound with her tongue, scanning her face, eyeing her. "I don't know what you were thinking. You could've been killed."

"Don't remind me." Emma groaned, darting her glance for a second to Melanie, then away again. "I'm clearly aware of my lack of sound judgement at the moment."

Melanie gnawed on her bottom lip. "Umm..." She reached over, brushing Emma's messy and unkept hair out of her eyes.

Emma pushed Melanie's hand away. "Please stop meddling." It came out harsher than she anticipated. Great, now she was acting like a spoiled brat. *Pull it together. None of this is her fault.* She pinched the bridge of her nose. "Sorry. I didn't mean for that to come out so harshly."

Attempting to smooth out her hair herself, she ran her hand over the top of her greasy and slick head. She reminded herself to remain calm and focus on her love for her and not her nonstop pandering. Since Jake left her high and dry, her mom's hovering had reached an astronomical level.

Emma pursed her lips together then tried her best to lower her tone as she said, "I didn't realize how fast I was going. I know it could've been much worse, but I'm grateful I'll recover fine. I guess that's my silver lining."

Squeezing her hands together, Melanie paused. "Well..." She glanced around before she settled into the chair next to her hospital bed. "The doctor said you need to stay overnight to be monitored. I already called your dad and updated him on the whole ordeal. He's relieved, to say the least. He almost drove up here..." She waved off the idea. "But I reassured him we'll be just fine. We only have another day left. No use in making a whole thing over it."

"Agreed." Last thing Emma needed was *two* parents watching her every move. "Thanks for talking him out of coming."

The pounding in her head made it difficult for her to concentrate on the conversation any longer. "I'm sorry, mom. I really am." Her voice lower and softer. "I wish this trip had gone differently, but thanks for coming with me." Emma forced a smile.

Melanie reached out, patting the top of her hand. "Anytime, honey."

Emma struggled to stay awake. "Mom, I'm *so* tired..." Her voice trailed off.

"Of course, you are. What a day you've had." Melanie jumped up, reaching for the light switch. "Let me dim the lights a little."

Relieved, she sighed. "Thanks mom." Emma wiggled around in her bed, struggling to find a comfortable position. Sean popped back into her mind. "What happened to the hot guy?" Her voice was low and weak, eyelids extra heavy.

"Sean?" Melanie smiled with approval, wagging her finger. "He's easy on the eyes, isn't he? I mean, he's practically dreamy." Smirking, she continued. "A real gentleman, that one."

"Mom!" Emma eyed Melanie. "Are you trying to date him?" she teased.

Melanie laughed. "I can see you haven't lost your sense of humor." She rolled her eyes. "Of course not. I'm happily married to your father... but anyone with eyes can see that man is one nice, cool glass of water."

Emma groaned, though her mom seemed to be reading her mind, and every woman's mind on planet earth for that matter.

"Sean was quite the knight in shining armor," Melanie declared. "He had me follow him here so I wouldn't get lost. Then he stayed until I found out you were okay, because he didn't want me to be alone if I received bad news."

Interest piqued. She knew from the moment she laid eyes on Sean he was nothing like Jake, which was a compliment of the highest kind. Jake could eat mud. "You don't say..." responded Emma.

Relaxing, Melanie leaned back in her chair. "I found out he's a veterinarian." She raised an eyebrow. "It's practically written in their DNA that they're nice."

Veterinarian? Sean was moving up on her imaginary checklist. A profession which she believed perfectly suited him. From the minute Sean crouched in front of her in the snowbank, she sensed he was a good guy. One of the few still out there, or so it seemed, in the desert wasteland of single men in their 30s.

"Veterinarian." She leaned her head back on the pillow, placing her hands on her stomach. "Makes sense."

A grin filled with mischief creeped across Melanie's face.

"He even gave me his business card to his clinic, in case we needed anything else while we're in town."

Smiling, Emma attempted to hide her pleasure in finding out this news. "I doubt we'll need anything..." She yawned. Mind foggy, her eyes flickered open and shut. "But... it was very thoughtful of him." Then she drifted off to sleep.

The shaking of her arm jarred her awake. Her eyes flipped open.

"I need to check your vitals." The no nonsense nurse placed her arm into the pressure sleeve.

Throat dry, she pushed herself up, searching for water. After taking a swig from the water bottle next to the hospital bed, Emma asked, "How long was I asleep?"

"No idea..." The nurse removed the pressure sleeve. "But we have to come in every thirty minutes to check your vitals."

Nodding, Emma scanned the small hospital room. Melanie was awake, reading a book. She remained quiet while the nurse finished.

Once the nurse left, Emma spoke up. "I'm feeling much better."

Closing her e-reader, Melanie reached over and patted the top of her knee. "I'm glad to hear it."

The events of the day had allowed Emma a small reprieve from thinking about Jake. Suddenly, it came crashing back down on her. The familiar weight was heavy and unbearable. "What am I going to do?" She flopped her arms down dramatically on top of the blanket.

"What do you mean?" Melanie raised an eyebrow. She sorted through her purse to find a nail file and settled into her chair, filing her nails.

"With my life..." Pinching the bridge of her nose, Emma tried to keep the tears forming at bay. "What... what am I going to do with my life? I'm returning to my job on Monday. Everyone's going to know what *happened*. It's mortifying."

She loudly inhaled. "I don't think I can handle everyone's questions. It's all too much."

Melanie stopped filing her nail, locking eyes with her. "You don't owe anyone an explanation." She glanced back down at her nails. Then she began to file another nail. "I'm sorry to tell you this, honey, but everyone already knows what happened." She blew off some nail dust.

Emma groaned. "You think everyone already knows?"

Melanie froze. "Come on." She raised an eyebrow. "News like yours? Spreads like wildfire."

"Ahhh," Emma wailed, "I hate my life!"

Quickly, she tossed her nail file back into her purse then waved her hands. "Enough of this pity party. There's somebody out there for you who is way better than Jake. Quit wasting your time on him. Good riddance."

With gritted teeth, Emma said, "That's easy for you to say. You didn't love him. I did."

"True... but I never liked him. I'm glad I never have to see him again."

Wanting to scream, she threw her face into her hands. "Mom... you've made your feelings abundantly clear." She peeked up. "You've reminded me of it multiple times since he left me."

Unfortunately, Emma hadn't listened to anyone's advice when it came to Jake. Filled with regret, she had looked past all the red flags, not wanting to believe she had chosen wrong. She devoted too much of her life to loving him. In her naïve, love can conquer all, attitude, she glossed over his innumerable flaws. Through her pain, she realized the error of her ways. If there was ever a next time, and that was a big *if*, she wouldn't be so reckless. She'd be smarter, less needy.

"Jake never appreciated you, but enough about Jake." Her jaw locked and eyes narrowed. She paused then cleared her throat. "Tomorrow, when you get out of this place, we're making a stop to thank Sean in person. We need to pick up some sort of gift. Giving someone a gift always makes these things easier and less awkward." She tapped her bottom lip with her pointer finger.

"I don't disagree with you. I do think we should stop by to thank him." Emma didn't add she wouldn't mind getting a second look at Sean. Tilting her head toward her, she continued, "But no scheming. You promise?"

Melanie held up both her hands. "Of course not."

Emma crossed her arms. "I mean it. It was nice of him to help me, and that's the only reason we're going by to thank him."

"Whatever you say, dear." Her voice indicated she had a different plan brewing.

Exasperated, Emma plopped her head back on her pillow. "Agreed. The discussion is over." She closed her eyes. Her mind was fuzzy again. "Could you let me rest for the thirty whole minutes I have before they wake me up again?"

"You bet." Melanie stood and flipped off the lights.

Emma began to drift off to sleep. Was she losing it? By agreeing to her mom's idea to stop by Sean's clinic, she knew she was opening a door to her mom's plotting. Maybe this concussion had messed with her ability to make rational choices? Sean and his blue dazzling eyes lingered at the forefront of her mind. Nah, it was she who wanted a second peek.

* * *

Standing next to the reception desk in his veterinarian clinic, Sean asked, "Julie, when's my next client coming in?" He glanced at his watch.

Julie had been a faithful employee of his dad for almost thirty years, and when he took over the clinic from him, he had kept her on. She was getting up in years and getting closer to retirement, and he dreaded the day when she would leave him. Over the years, since he had no contact with his mom, Julie had acted like a second mom. With kids grown and out of the house, she now used all her maternal energy to give him unsolicited advice.

Julie peered up from her computer screen. "You have Mr. Martin and his lab coming in ten minutes."

He eyed his watch again, quickly trying to calculate how long it took to walk a few doors down Main Street and back. "I was hoping to have time to run to the pharmacy to pick up the medicine for Ms. Pinner's cat. I told her I'd drop it off after work today." He shifted the clipboard he was holding to his other hand. "I don't think I can squeeze it in before Mr. Martin gets here."

Scanning her computer screen, Julie made a few clicks with her mouse, then pointed at the screen. "After Mr. Martin checks in, we won't have anyone till after lunch. I can run and get it right after I check him in."

Sean smiled. "Perfect. I don't know what I would do without you."

A mischievous smile crossed her face. "This place would fall apart, and you'd miss me. Then you'd realize I was the best employee you'd ever had."

"That's definitely correct." Sean laughed. Looking down at his clipboard, he made a final note on the chart. Once done, he unclipped it and handed it to Julie. "This is the chart for Ms. Summers' labradoodle."

Julie took the chart from him. "No problem. I'll enter the information right now."

Before pivoting to head back to his office, something caught Sean's eye. He swore he saw Emma with her mom pass by his clinic's windows. His heart began a steady rise in his chest. Squinting, he narrowed his eyes to confirm his suspicion. Before he had a chance to study them, they disappeared from his view. He took a few steps toward the window, peering in their direction. The pulsing of his temples made him all aware of his piqued interest in Emma. A woman he barely knew, but apparently found intriguing.

The women pivoted on their feet and headed back in the direction of his clinic. Sean got a better view of them and confirmed it was Emma and Melanie. Emma looked even more beautiful than the day before, when most of her was covered in snow and snow gear. Today, she had her hair down, loose and wavy, hitting the middle of her shoulder blades. Her jeans hugged her in all the right places, while her green sweater under her jacket, accentuated her brilliant hazel eyes. He hated how much he noticed the gracefully sway of her hips. Swiftly, Sean stepped back to avoid them spotting him snooping at them through the window.

Then, without warning, Emma opened the clinic door and popped her head in, scanning the waiting room. Her gaze caught him, smiling. "Sean! Good morning." She fully pushed the door open and strode into the clinic with Melanie in tow.

His palms started to sweat, heart racing faster than a sprinter. Warmness pooled in his stomach. All this from a woman he met yesterday. *Calm down, boy.*

Wiping her feet on the doormat inside, she made a quick survey of the room. Then out of breath, she said, "I'm glad we found the right place."

His voice was unsteady when he finally replied, "Emma... Melanie...?" His eyes widened, sweeping over Emma. Drinking her all in, wishing he was a smoother talker and not a jumbled mess in her presence. "What are you two doing here? Is everything okay?"

Tongue-tied, he found it hard to think of anything else to say. He met people all day long and had a great ability to make small talk with his clients. Not Emma. She made his mouth dry and mind blank.

"Sean, it's good to see you again." Melanie closed the space between them. Emma followed, edging closer to him.

Glancing over his shoulder, he made eye contact with Julie. She smirked, but remained stoically silent. Quickly, he brought his attention back to the two women, stepping toward them. Swallowing down the lump in his throat, he willed himself to pull it together. "How are you feeling Emma?" He managed.

"Much better. Thanks." Smiling, Emma held out a paper bag to him. "I wanted to come by to thank you for all your help yesterday. You really went above and beyond. This is a small gift of gratitude."

His eyes locked with hers, making his chest tighten from her unrestrained glance. "That's very... nice of you. Completely unnecessary, but nevertheless, thank you." He took the bag from her.

Shoving one hand into the pocket of her jeans, Emma bit down on her bottom lip. "I didn't know what to get you." She glanced sideways at Melanie, then brought her gaze back to him. She wrung her hands. "I picked up some pastries at the bakery down the street. Again... only a small thank you for your help yesterday."

Clearing his throat, he smiled. "Thanks. I love Pops Pies. This was very thoughtful of you." He gestured, shaking the bag.

Melanie stepped closer. "No, Sean really, I'm so appreciative of everything you did. From helping me find the hospital, to staying with me until I knew Emma was going to be okay. I won't ever forget how kind you were. Thanks again."

Shrugging, he brushed off their comments. "It was nothing. I was glad I could help." He smiled again, puffing up his chest.

Julie cleared her throat. Sean pivoted, pointing over his

shoulder with his thumb. "This is my secretary, Julie." He grinned. "She keeps this placing running."

Julie raised her hand in a wave. "Nice to meet both of you."

Pointing at her chest, Emma said, "Likewise. I'm Emma." She gestured toward Melanie. "This is my mom, Melanie. We met Sean yesterday, skiing at Bluebird Mountain."

"Is that right...?" Julie's stare darted back and forth between them, her voice lingering extra-long on the last word.

Ignoring Julie's innuendo, Sean closed his eyes for a brief moment, before he continued. "How much longer are you in town?"

"We head back tomorrow." Emma shifted her weight, adjusting her purse strap. "Today is our last day, which to me is a relief. This wasn't exactly the vacation I had planned." Forcing a smile, her lips formed a tight line. "Thanks again." She held her hand up in a wave then pivoted to leave.

Without thought, and against his better judgement, because Sean didn't want this to be the last time he ever saw Emma, he said, "Let me take you two out tonight." He bravely met her gaze, making the air around him heavy. "It's your last night, and I know the best place to eat."

"Umm..." Emma shuffled her feet. "I don't know what we have planned."

Melanie smirked, then she replied, "I have plans to meet up with an old friend who lives here, so I'm busy. I can't."

Shaking her head, Emma paused pursing her lips together.

He boldly pressed forward. "Emma, are you busy, too?" Waiting for a reply, he fiddled with his hands.

Emma exchanged a quick look with her mom before she tilted her head toward him. "I'm... I'm not busy."

He swallowed, willing himself to not chicken out. To not live anymore with regrets. "I'd love to still take you out even though your mom's busy.... that is, if it's okay with you?"

Emma nodded, fluffing her hair. "I guess that could work."

Sean knew her heart was shattered, being jilted practically at the altar. If anything, this dinner would never lead to more. Something which oddly catapulted him forward. Maybe it was the lack of pressure? With his over eager hero complex, he felt equipped to help her mend her broken heart.

"Does six o'clock work?" asked Sean.

Emma tightly smiled. "Sure... That works... Do you have a pen for me to write down the address of where we're staying?"

"I have one." Piped up Julie, who had remained quiet but gleefully watched the entire interaction. "Here." She held out a pen.

"Thanks Julie, but I've got one right here." Reaching into his shirt pocket, he pulled one out and held it out to Emma.

"Thanks." Her eyes glimmered back at him, taking it from his hand.

Sean scanned the top of the reception desk for a piece of paper.

Reading his mind, Julie grabbed a pad of sticky notes, holding it out to him with a smirk. "Here. You can use this."

"Thanks." Sean grabbed the pad, ignoring her obvious look. "Here you go."

"Okay..." Emma quickly wrote down her number and address of the resort. "It's nearby." She handed him back the pad and pen.

He read the address. "I know the place." He brightly smiled. "I'll see you tonight."

"Sounds like a plan." Emma moved toward the door, lingering on the threshold. "Until then."

"Bye." Sean replied.

Emma and Melanie exited.

Playing with the notepad and pen, Sean waited for his

heart rate to return to normal speed. Once it settled, he pivoted back, facing Julie. "What?" he asked.

Julie grinned. "Nothing." She shook her head and peered back at her computer screen.

"Come on... out with it." Sean knew she was dying to comment on the whole interaction she had witnessed. Julie had seen him date many women over the years. She didn't mince words when she disapproved of one of them.

Raising an eyebrow, she shifted in her chair. "Emma's the woman you helped at the resort?"

"Correct." Sean pulled the top sticky note off the pad, setting it back on Julie's desk. He folded the note, sticking it in his pocket.

The room filled with the sound of her keys clicking, she continued to type while she said, "when you told me the whole story earlier, you conveniently left out that the woman you helped was gorgeous."

He smirked. "Did I?"

Julie stopped typing, glancing over at him. "Yes." She made a tsk sound. "You made me think you had done your civic duty helping some poor old woman. Instead, you skillfully finagled your way into a date." Grinning, she rolled her eyes. "Figures."

Sean laughed. "Is that what I did?"

Though Julie was correct, none of that had been his intention from the beginning. Yesterday when he left the hospital, he believed that was the end of the story. Emma showing up at his office was a pleasant surprise.

Julie cleared her throat. "That's exactly what you did. I, for one, can't wait to see how all of this plays out."

Squaring his shoulders, Sean asked, "Do you get a kick out of my dating life?"

"You bet I do." Julie smiled, dramatically throwing her hands down on top of the desk. "Especially this time. I don't think I've ever seen you squirm or fumble over your words like you just did." She waved her finger in a circular motion. "You, my friend, have smitten kitten written all over your face." Julie cackled while she began to type once more.

Sean opened his mouth to respond, but had no words. Loudly exhaling, he pivoted on his foot, heading back to his office. What had he been thinking? Why was he wasting his time asking a woman out who didn't even live in Bluebird? Emma might live on the other side of the country for all he knew. She might be a city girl, while his whole life had been spent in this small country town.

Entering his office, he plopped himself down into his desk chair and leaned his elbows on the top of his desk, pondering his predicament. Why had he asked Emma out on a date? The answer was clear. Sean was drawn to her, wanting more time with her, even it was only for one dinner. None of it made sense.

Julie poked her head into the doorway of his office, interrupting his scattered thoughts. "Mr. Martin is here, lover boy." She held out the needed medical chart to him.

Sean glanced over at her, rolling his eyes. Julie was determined to make a fool out of him. "Very funny, Julie. But please... enough. This isn't a big deal."

He pushed himself up, striding toward Julie. Aggressively, he ripped the medical chart out of her hands.

Julie folded her arms. "Geez. A little testy are we." She slipped away back to reception. "I'll drop it." She stated over her shoulder.

Why was he acting so defensive? Julie always teased him about the women coming and going in his life, but this time she hit a nerve. It was only one date, right?

Chapter Four

Flat on her back, Emma laid on her hotel bed staring up at the ceiling. Slowly, she counted the ceiling tiles, distracting herself from any real reflection. Sean kept running rampant through her mind. She wondered why she had agreed to go on a date him, because she wasn't ready to date anyone. Who knew when she would be?

Every waking minute of her day replayed her entire relationship with Jake on an endless loop. Looking for hidden clues or signs she should've seen, but didn't. It was agony. A type of pain she would never wish on anyone, even her worst enemy. Why had she believed Jake loved her? The whole ordeal had completely shattered her belief that she was capable of making a sound judgement. If she could fall for a guy who never loved her, what would keep her from repeating the same mistake with someone else?

Tears stung her eyes, cascading down her cheeks. Jake. Jake. Jake. The man might have ruined her for all future men. The thought made her grit her teeth in anger.

"Sean's going to be here in an hour, and you're a complete

mess." Melanie walked across the room and whacked Emma on her thigh. "Stop your moping. You've a date with a handsome vet. Now pull yourself together. I refuse to let you waste your life away thinking about Jake." She towered over her with a hand on her hip.

"I'm not going." Emma lifted her arm, covering her eyes to block out the overhead light. Even if Sean was smoking hot with his big ole baby blues, none of it mattered.

Melanie whacked her on the thigh once more, grabbing her arm off her face. She leaned over her, her face inches from her own. "Emma..." Her tone was softer. "Things will get better, but you'll have to at least try."

Unflinching, she stared back at her and said, slowly, emphasis added to each word, "I am *not* going."

"Oh yes, you are." Melanie exhaled, pinching the bridge of her nose. Emma knew her patience was wearing thin. "I don't know how else to help you, but in your current state of feeling sorry for yourself, I realize it's more imperative than ever you go on this date. If only to restore your faith in men." She paused and held out her hand to help Emma sit up. "It's only one date, Emma. Nobody's proposing marriage. You'll get to face the demons at home soon enough. Why don't you allow yourself a break from your wallowing?"

Emma didn't reach out to take her hand, so Melanie grabbed both of her hands with her own, pulling her limp and lifeless body forward into a sitting position.

"Fine." Emma stood up, marching to the bathroom. She glanced over her shoulder before entering and said, "I can guarantee that I won't like a minute of it." She slammed the door behind her.

"Fine." Melanie yelled. "I'm holding you to that."

Once in the solitude of the bathroom, Emma leaned forward, gripping the edge of the bathroom sink with both hands. At one time, she had been cute and likeable, not now. Recoiling at her reflection, she was a mere shell of her former self. Her eyes were dark and sunken. The dark circles under her puffy eyes reconfirmed her worst nightmare.

"Pull yourself together," she ordered her reflection, taking a deep breath. Tears stinging her eyes, she quickly wiped them away. Someday she might not have a heart full of despair. Unfathomable, but possible. She continued, "You can do this. A nice and good-looking guy asked you out."

With nothing left to do, she gathered an outfit from her suitcase, throwing it on. The image of herself slightly better. Lately, her sweatpants had become her one and only outfit of choice. A change of clothes on, she applied some makeup, not for Sean, but for herself. It was essential she brighten her dull appearance, restore herself to some semblance of the person she was only the month prior. A person who was happy and carefree.

While she finished getting ready, she forced herself to not think about Jake for a solid ten minutes, which proved to be incredibly difficult. Once done, she stepped back and took in the whole sight of herself. A smile crept across her face. "You can do this," she repeated out loud, to her new, better-looking image.

Melanie was on the bed watching T.V. when Emma made her appearance from the bathroom. She peered over at her, smiling. "You look great." She hit the mute button on the remote and she continued, "better than you have in weeks."

"You think so?" Nervously, Emma smoothed the front of her outfit with her hand. It had been years since she had been on a first date. The thought made her feel sick to her stomach.

Melanie gave a curt nod. "Yes. You look beautiful."

"Thanks." Emma sat on the edge of the bed, fiddling with her watch. "He should be here any minute. When are you meeting up with your nonexistent friends?"

With a wave of her hand, Melanie chuckled. "Later. I'll walk into town after you leave and grab something to eat."

Exhaling, Emma ringed her shaky hands together. "I can't believe we go home tomorrow... back to reality, I guess." She willed herself to not panic at the thought.

Melanie reached over, giving her shoulder a squeeze. "Only good things to come." Her eyes locked with hers. "Promise. You've got your whole life ahead of you. Plenty of time to find someone new. Plus, Jake did you a favor. Could you imagine being married to someone who didn't love you?" She made a tsk sound with her tongue, shaking her head. Then she tilted her head forward. "At least he backed out before the wedding, not after."

Had he done her a favor? Probably. The only thing pushing her forward was the hope things would improve with time. Her hope being each day, she would think about him less and less. Then perhaps one day, she wouldn't think about him at all.

Emma stared blankly at the muted T.V. and mulled over her mom's words. "You're probably right." She shifted, glancing back at her. "But..." She stuttered. "But... I still can't imagine there ever being another guy for me."

If Jake wasn't the one for her, then who was? How could she ever trust herself to find someone new? She thought Jake was the one and look how that ended.

A knock on the door interrupted her thoughts. Both exchanged a look.

Melanie spoke up, "You'd better get that. Your handsome man awaits. I hope you can forget about your broken heart, even if it's for one night and have a nice time."

"I hope so, too." Emma pushed herself off the bed to answer the door.

Swinging open the door, the tangy scent of his cologne hit her nostrils. The tantalizing fumes danced around her, making it hard for her to concentrate. Sean glanced up from where he stood. He looked even better than she remembered. This time in his casual slacks and blue button-down shirt. A shirt which made his eyes pop, reflecting every speck of blue in the universe. Her stomach did a flip-turn. A surprise, being Jake hadn't caused that sort of reaction for her in years.

"Sean... Hi." Emma managed. Her voice was shaky, revealing her nerves.

"Emma." Sean shoved his hands into his pockets. He paused for a moment. A smile creeping across his ruggedly handsome face. "You look... fantastic."

Fresh heat splashed her cheeks. "I... don't... Thanks." She fumbled over her words. It had been a long time since a man had complimented her on her looks. Jake had never been good at telling her she was beautiful. She peered down at her black sweater and white slacks, then brought her gaze back to his. Eyes locked, her mouth suddenly became dry. "You clean up nice yourself."

Sean grinned. "I appreciate the compliment." He looked over her shoulder into the hotel room. "Hi. Melanie." He waved.

Melanie waved back. "Nice to see you again, Sean. You two have a nice time."

He nodded, then ran his eyes back to Emma. "You ready to go? We'll just walk since it's down the street." Sean took a step closer to her, lightly touching her on the forearm. He crossed their physical barrier, and though she had on a sweater, his touch burned through the fabric spreading its warmth all the way up her arm.

She gulped. "Walk... sure." She was unnerved from his simple touch.

Worry flashed across his face. "Unless that's not okay. You're cleared by the doctor to walk a few blocks, right?"

Emma forced herself to answer. "I can walk. Let me grab my jacket." Reaching into the room, she held the door open with her other hand. She grabbed her jacket off the chair next to the door. "Bye, mom." She whispered.

Emma closed the door behind her, nervously tucking her hair behind her ears.

Sean pointed to the left. "Right this way. It's a little past my clinic. The restaurant has the best Italian food. Do you even like Italian food?" He bit down on his bottom lip. She smiled, realizing Sean was nervous. The man was human. "I guess I should've asked beforehand what type of food you preferred." He ran a hand through his dark locks.

The gesture lessened the tightness in her own chest, warming her to her core. She reached out, placing her hand on his forearm. "Sounds great. I'm not picky."

They continued toward the restaurant, falling in step with one another. On their walk, they passed all the little shops which attracted the tourists. The chocolate shop, souvenir shop, ice cream, and loads of restaurants.

Though Bluebird wasn't large, it was quaint and had grown on her during the week. If she hadn't been so depressed, she imagined she would have enjoyed walking Main Street more than she did during her stay. The last bit of sunlight slipped away, and darkness settled upon them. The streetlamps which lined the sidewalk kicked on. The whole area became cozy as a warm glow danced across Sean's eyes. Taunting and twinkling back at her, they made her forget all about Jake.

A silence lingered between them. Emma worried the night would be filled with awkward and painful moments. She wracked her brain for something to ask. "Did you like growing up here?" She tilted her head to the side, waiting for his response.

He scratched his head. "Did I like growing up here?" Sean gave a forced laugh. "Kind of a loaded question." He shoved his hands into his pockets.

Studying his face and broad shoulders, she willed herself to focus on his eyes and not his chiseled jawline. "Is it? I..." She worried she had stumbled into unwarranted territory. "I only wanted to get to know you a little better."

Sean stopped walking and rubbed the back of his neck. "Sorry..." He shifted his weight. "I know you didn't mean anything by it... I apologize. Let's just say my growing up... my formative years were less than ideal."

"I'm sorry to hear that." Emma stated, knowing she had walked her way into a part of his life he preferred to keep private.

Sean tilted his body closer to her. He and Emma fell into step once more.

"It was fine to grow up here," he continued, "but... honestly, I couldn't wait to leave when I turned eighteen. I thought I was missing out, being trapped in this little town. I had an unquenchable urge to get out and spread my wings. Then once I went to college then vet school, I was ready to come back to the place which had always been home."

Emma studied him. "Were your parents from here, too?"

His jaw locked. Eyes narrowed. Sean inhaled and his eyes swept to hers. "My dad was from here." After a few beats of time, he continued. "My mom wasn't from here, and she never liked it." He fidgeted with the button on his overcoat. "Actually... she hated it and complained about it until she moved. Claimed this wasn't the place or life she wanted, including my dad and myself." Shrugging his shoulders, they dropped a few noticeable inches.

She cleared her throat, fully aware she stumbled upon a sensitive topic. "What about other family? Do they all live in Bluebird, too?"

Sean shook his head. "No. They have long since passed away."

Maybe it was the romantic lighting or the way his voice cracked a little when he mentioned his mom, but Emma reached out and looped her arm around his. She held on as they continued toward the restaurant. "So... is it just you and your dad? Any siblings?"

"Nope, no siblings. It's always been me and my dad. My mom left us when I was eleven." He cleared his throat, kept his eyes straight ahead. "I haven't seen her since then."

"Eleven," repeated Emma. "That's heavy. I'm so sorry. That must've been horrible for you."

Sean patted the top of her hand, then abruptly stopped. "Many have had it way worse than me. We're here."

Emma let go of his arm, walking through the door he held open for her. The door closed behind them, shutting off the topic of his mom with it.

* * *

The two lingered in the crowded waiting room for their table to be ready. Too loud to talk, both stood close to one another in silence. Darting his eyes away from hers, Sean told himself not to stare at Emma the entire time. Being in her presence did something to him, and he couldn't think straight. Somehow, he rambled on too much, revealing way more than he wanted. Right out of the gate, he told her all about his mom. Once he dated a woman a full year before he ever divulged about his mom leaving him. What was wrong with him? Surely, the situation had made Emma feel awkward. He had willed himself to stop or change the subject, yet he failed. Crashed and burned, when it came to her, he became loose lipped.

Even now, her arm inches from his was making his middle molten lava. They weren't even touching! None of this was feasible. In the past, he had always managed to maintain a clear head with women. This whole situation terrified him. Emma had already carefully unwrapped the deepest parts of him. The parts he kept locked up, but with her rules begone. He trusted Emma. Why? He'd personally love to know the answer.

The hostess called their name, interrupting his thoughts. Glancing at Emma, he smiled. "Please... you first." He placed his hand on the small of her back, holding his other arm out in a gesture for her to follow the hostess.

Emma returned his smile, gazing up at him. "Thanks."

The hostess led them to a booth at the front, facing the huge windows overlooking Main Street. It was his favorite spot in the entire place. From the table, one had a perfect view of the people walking by. A bonus was it was located next to the cozy fireplace, which warmed him all the way to his core.

Emma peered up from her menu. "What do you usually get here?" Her eyes sparkled, reflecting the light from the candle center piece. "Any suggestions?" She pulled her glance back down to the menu.

Sean shifted, forcing himself to concentrate on their conversation and not on the perfect way her hair had fallen over her shoulders. Clearing his throat, he responded, "everything's good here, but I usually get the Bolognese or fettucine Alfredo."

Emma padded her bottom lip with her fingers. "Those both sound delicious. I haven't had much of an appetite lately." Exhaling, her eyes flickered across his own. "I've been a bit out of sorts."

"That's understandable." He stated, wanting nothing more than to swipe away the pain which had seeped across her face.

Emma gave a curt nod, biting her bottom lip. Sadness clouded her eyes.

"Order both things if you like." Sean blurted out. Anything to cheer up her disposition, because he knew she was thinking of the other guy. The one who left. "One for now, and one for you to take home. Then you can eat it tomorrow."

Her eyes brightened with the suggestion. "Really? Are you sure?"

Sean sighed, relieved to see her happy. "Positive. Order both, and I'll do the same. I live alone and don't cook. I can eat it tomorrow for dinner, too." He closed his menu, resting his hands on top.

Grinning, Emma threw her hands up. "You've convinced me. I'll get both." Closing her menu, she reached out and grabbed her glass of water, taking a sip. "I might as well eat and be happy."

Smirking, Sean reached out and gave her hand a quick squeeze. "Now that's the spirit." He let go.

Emma laughed. A sound more beautiful than ocean waves. Pleased with himself, because he had brought some happiness to her life, even for a few minutes. Something he was positive had been nonexistent in her life over the last few weeks. Shifting in his seat, he pulled his shoulders back. The server came back, and placed their order.

Once alone again, Sean asked, "What do you think of Bluebird? Have you enjoyed your time here?" He cringed, immediately regretting the question. Emma was on a failed honeymoon trip with her mom. Surely, the trip had been less than enjoyable. "I... I mean..."

Emma became quiet. She tilted her head toward the window, staring at the people passing by. She exhaled. Her shoulders drooping. "Bluebird is a truly magical place. It's why I selected it for my honeymoon." A look of defeat took up residence on her face. "If the circumstances had been different, I imagine this place would've grown on me." She turned her head back to face him. Her look rattled him, throwing him off course. "Now, all I want to do is go home. Not that home will be any better." Sadness rippled across her eyes, while she gnawed on her bottom lip.

Without a thought, he reached out across the table, grabbing her hand. "I'm sorry I brought that up." Lightly, he squeezed her hand. She didn't pull away, but she squeezed his hand back. The air in between them sizzled and crackled, at least it did for him. Gulping, he mustered up courage to continue. "I know it'll get easier with time, and eventually you'll find someone new. Then you'll forget all about him." He let go of her hand. Moving his hands under the table, he wrung them together.

Maybe he could be the guy to help her move on. Why? Beats him. He was the king of no commitment, but he believed Emma would be worth the risk. *Whoa, back up. The woman is telling you she has a broken heart. Listen.*

Shaking her head, she ran her eyes to the window. "One could certainly hope. The alternative of ending up alone is surely depressing." The words lingered. Words he imagined played on repeat in her mind.

Sean pulled his hands from under the table, resting his elbows on it with fingers steepled. "Hey..." He tried to find the right words. "Someone like you..." He drank her all in, making his temples pulsate. His body ignited. "You'll never end up alone." He boldly stated.

Her eyes widened. A light flickered across them, an awakening of sorts. "Sean, you think it's possible? Possible in a world of billions of people to find love twice?" Her eyes misty, she glanced down. "I really loved him."

"I'm sure you did." He agreed.

Wiping her eyes, Emma stared back at him. "I don't know if I'll ever find that type of love again."

Sean almost laughed. The idea of *the one* and seemed ludicrous. "Don't be ridiculous." He waved off her comment. "You'll find love again. Have you looked at yourself lately?" He raised an eyebrow. "Because... you are gorgeous. You're everyone's type."

Her cheeks reddened at his compliment. "I don't know about that."

"Okay... maybe not everyone's type, but nobody is, but close." He waved a finger at her. "Don't sell yourself short. Things can only get better from here."

For whatever reason, his words must have done the trick, because Emma burst out laughing. "They certainly can only get better." Wide eyes, she covered her mouth with her hand.

Sean grinned. "See you're feeling better already."

A look of optimism flashed across her face. "I am." She exhaled, smiling. "Thanks."

"Absolutely." Sean nodded to reassure her.

Who was he? He wasn't a guy who believed in love. If anything, he was the guy who believed nobody stayed together. Life always found a way to pull people apart. Marriage, half the time, ended up in divorce. With both parties involved, hashing it out in court over the summer home in the Hamptons. Though he believed full heartily in his level of cynicism, he found it oddly refreshing that Emma still believed the opposite. The oil to his vinegar.

The server interrupted their discussion, bringing their food to the table. Determined to change the subject to something more jovial, Sean pivoted them in a different direction. Away from the Emma's ill-fated love story.

Sean speared his chicken Alfredo, taking a bite. Shifting, he leaned forward, wiping his mouth. "Enough about all that... tell me about your job. Melanie mentioned you were a teacher?"

A splash of light skidded across her eyes, and Emma

smiled. "I've taught third grade since I graduated from college. I love that age. The kids are so curious and are learning new things at an exhilarating pace." She broke off a piece of bread and chewed.

His eyes found hers and for a few thumps of his heart, he didn't look away. "I'm sure the kids love you," added Sean.

"I hope so." Emma tilted her head, her gaze making his skin sizzle. "What were you like in school?"

"In elementary school?" He laughed, remembering what a jokester he was back then. He was positive his teachers dreaded having him in class. A lot of it was a cry for attention, since he received zero at home. Once his mom left, his dad became a closed off and absent parent. In some ways, he lost both at the same time. It wasn't until he was in high school, with a heart full of anger and resentment, that his dad finally started being his dad again.

Sean teased, "You're going to hate me when I tell you."

Emma chuckled. "Let me guess..." She raised an eyebrow. "You were the class clown."

"Guilty." Sean took a sip of his water. "Unfortunately, I probably gave my teachers a real run for their money."

She nodded. "I definitely have a few of those. Nothing I can't handle. Those kids keep me on my toes." Tilting her head to the side, she examined him. "How were you when you were a teenager? Did you settle down a bit?"

Sean tried to remember himself as a child. Before his mom left, he had been secure and well-behaved. It was like a bait and switch once she was gone. He desperately wanted attention, and he was willing to look for it by any means possible. By high school, he accepted his fate, then his sole focus became leaving Bluebird. To prove to himself, he was better than his mom believed to him, a person who was worthy of love.

He cleared his throat, tugging at his collar. "I was loads

better in high school. Believe it or not, I received good grades. By then, I was highly motivated to get myself out of Bluebird. I knew A's were my one ticket out of this town."

With a smile, she asked, "It worked, right?"

Nodding, he remembered how driven he was to leave. "Yes, true. I went away for college..." He paused, thinking of the day he drove away with all his belongings packed into the back seat of his car. Right before he left, Sean had a huge fight with his dad. With a heart full of anger, for years of not having his mom, for his dad being constantly distant, he said a lot of things he regretted. Luckily, he later realized his dad had done the best he could. After all, he was the parent who had stayed. The one who loved him even if he had a hard time showing it. He cringed at how he acted. "In college, I figured out who I wanted to be, then came to realize Bluebird wasn't as bad as I remembered."

Emma nodded. "Isn't that how it always goes? Blame our parents for everything, only to realize they wanted what was best for us all along?"

"Certainly." Sean shifted in his seat. "At least I can say that's true about my dad."

Emma's gaze skidded across him. His heart studiedly rose to a brisk pace. "I'm glad you have your dad. That's more than I can say for some of the children in my class. As a teacher, I see the gamut of parents. Some of the circumstances these children come from are truly heartbreaking... you... you're lucky you had *someone*."

Sean gulped, nodding. "True. It's more than others." He tried to read the range of emotions written on her face. Emma had a level of compassion which wasn't lost on him. She was different, deeper, more thoughtful than any of the other women he had met in the past. It was refreshing.

For the rest of dinner, the conversation flowed between

them like he was talking to an old friend. He learned she was from a town about an hour away in Vermont. College had been in Boston. An east coast girl through and through.

As dinner wrapped up, he found himself not wanting the night to end. Honestly, he couldn't remember a time when he had a conversation as easy and effortless as the one he was having with her. The server boxed up their extra dinner each, then he wracked his brain for something to extend the night.

"Would you mind if I take you to one more place?" He knew it was getting late, but tomorrow she would be gone. If this was the only date he would experience with Emma, he wanted to soak up every minute he had left.

Emma smiled. "Sure."

"Great. Let's go." Sean slipped out of the booth, following behind her.

As they exited, the cold winter air bit at their skin. Emma buttoned up her jacket and wrapped a scarf around her neck. Clearly shivering, Sean peeled off his overcoat, placing it around her shoulders.

"Are you sure?" Her eyes danced to his, searching for confirmation. "It's freezing out here."

Sean readjusted the jacket, hanging it properly over her shoulders. "Positive." Smiling, he reluctantly removed his hands. It was difficult. He had caught a whiff of her perfume, and it was making him dizzy. His mind ran rampant at the idea of her hair between his fingertips. He cleared his throat, lying through his teeth. "I'm used to this weather, and I'm warm blooded." He was freezing, and it took everything within him to keep his teeth from chattering. But all that mattered was if she was warm.

Emma pulled the coat tighter against her body. "Thanks. That's very kind of you. I appreciate it." She smiled, making him straighten his back.

He shrugged, plunging his hands into his pockets as they continued down Main Street. They passed the shops and restaurants. "I'd like to take you to this place I always used to go as a teenager at night, when I didn't want to go home. Would it be okay if I showed you?" asked Sean.

Emma's cheeks were rosy, and pink tinged her nose. "Sounds nice." Her voice sent a shiver down his spine.

Sean peeled his eyes away, glancing up the sidewalk. "It's not too far. I promise."

Main Street still had all the Christmas lights up, and they twinkled and danced in the windows of the shops. Just as the path of Main Street ended, it curved up a small road which led to a little hill overlooking town. Tucked away at the top, was a small park with a few benches. Often in the summer, families picnicked on the crisp green grass under the shade of the pine trees. The place was the keeper of many happy memories for Sean. The ones before, when his family was complete, when his mom was still in his life. Times when he still felt loved.

The summer before his mom abandoned him, his family had taken a picnic up to the park right as the sun was setting on the horizon. Just the three of them were in the park that evening, and they ate fried chicken straight from the big round paper bucket. After they stuffed themselves with chicken, his mom lounged on a blanket while he and his dad threw a football back and forth. He could still remember how the grass crunched beneath his bare feet, and the sound of his mom's laugh as she watched them. For just a speck of time, he had thought his family was whole. Little did he know how unhappy his mom had been, so unhappy that she would pack up and leave without a word a few months later. He was never the same.

Sean shook his head at the memory of it, willing himself to remain in the present with Emma. Wishing the memories of the past didn't taint his life like they did. As they entered the park, the night sky was void of a moon or stars. His eyes quickly adjusted to the dim lighting from the overhead park lights. Spotting a bench overlooking the town, he pointed. Emma followed him to the bench, settling down next to him. The view from where they sat overlooked the houses below and Main Street. Both took in the view.

Sean leaned closer to Emma, shoulders and elbows touching. "I haven't been here in a long time." He exhaled, pushing out the feelings trapped inside of him.

Emma raised the collar of his jacket, slipping her arms into it. She pulled it tight across her chest, holding it closed. "Why not?"

Sean spoke to the space in front of him. "As a child, right after my mom left, I used to come here all the time. I'd sit and stare out at all the houses down below. I liked to imagine the houses were filled with happy families. I wondered what they had for dinner. What movie they were watching together. Anything seemed more inviting than being in my apartment with my dad..." His voice trailed off, his jaw locking. All of it crashing down on him, making it hard for him to breathe. The painful memories of the past no longer carefully packed away, but instead were at the forefront with no place to hide.

"I can't imagine how difficult that must've been for you." She buried her hands into his jacket's pockets, pulling her gaze from the view to him. He met her glance, gulping. Her gaze seared his skin. The woman had an eerie ability to read him like a book. The feeling was uncanny, yet exhilarating. "I'm sorry you had to experience that kind of loss... and pain."

Sean refused to be the first to break the spell. His eyes flickering between her eyes and lips. The full luscious lips, and he wondered what it would feel like to kiss her. To allow his lips to part hers. Because he *wanted* to kiss her. *Look away.*

Look away. She gulped then reverted her glance back to the space in front of them. He followed her eyeline back to the town. Even now, after all these years, he rarely spoke about his mom. Things seemed different with Emma because she seemed equally aware of the pain and burden of a broken heart. A different type of broken heart from his, but nevertheless, broken.

He cleared his throat, speaking out to the houses in front of them. "You see, everything was so dark after my mom left. My dad became a complete mess, withdrawing from me, becoming a shell of his former self." He popped the collar of his sports coat, burying his hands into the pockets. "I felt like I lost them both. I once had everything... then I had nothing. I often wondered what I had done to break up our family. I wondered why I wasn't good enough to make her want to say. Of course, I didn't have any of the answers, so instead I'd come here and stare out at all those houses." He moved his arm in front of him, back and forth over the tops of the view. "I wanted to believe someday I could have a happy home like the ones below. I don't know if that even exists."

Though his mom left long ago, he had become hardened to the idea of happiness. Reminding himself constantly that nobody stayed. Nobody was truly happy. The picture others painted for those in public was rarely what was happening.

Emma placed her hand on top of his thigh. Her eyes danced to his. "You can still have all that." Her voice was serene, calm as the sea after a storm.

His mind went blank. All he could think of was her hand on his thigh. The heat from her touch spreading through his body. He found it hard to breathe. "I... I don't know what I believe in anymore."

Nodding, Emma bit her bottom lip. "I can sense that." She pulled her gaze away, removing her hand from his thigh.

Before she had time to continue, Sean twisted around, pointing in the direction of an icy hill covered in snow, wanting desperately to change the subject. "As a teenager, we used to sled down that hill right over there."

Emma raised an eyebrow, glancing over her shoulder toward the hill. "Isn't that kind of dangerous? That's a steep hill." She laughed nervously.

"Incredibly dangerous." He laughed, his gaze catching hers.

Grinning, she rolled her eyes. "I should've known." She glimmered from the illumination of the lamppost, relaxing the tension in between his shoulder blades. He hoped he helped her forget the mess of the last few weeks of her life. It took everything within him not to lean in and kiss her. Never had he wanted something more with anyone, but Sean pushed the ridiculous thought away. He couldn't kiss her. The woman had a broken heart. A romantic connection with him had to be the furthest thing from her mind. Too bad it was the *only* thing he could think about.

Teasingly, Sean bumped his shoulder against hers. "Aren't teenage boys born to do dumb, idiotic things in their youth?"

Emma exhaled, rolling her eyes. "Probably. It's amazing any of you make it to eighteen."

Sean grinned. "A true miracle."

The temperature had dropped even lower. Sean stood and extended a hand to help Emma up, suggesting they get Emma back to her hotel.

"I've kept you out in the cold long enough," he told her.

Falling into step with one another, Emma tilted her head toward him, smiling. Her eyes twinkled, taunting him more than she would ever know.

She pulled her gaze away from his and back to the path in front of them. "You've helped me forget for a bit about what's really going on in my life. I appreciate it. I'm glad I met you, Sean." Her voice lingered over his name.

He gulped. His hands clammy. "Likewise." His pulse quickened. Emma made the world tilt off course. She made him wish for a moment to have someone special in his life. He brushed it all off, pushing the thought a thousand miles away.

Eventually, their feet hit the cobblestone paved path of Main Street. It was worn smooth from hundreds of years of use. Their shoulders bumped as they squeezed next to each other, allowing others to pass on the narrow sidewalk. It was intimate; the nearness weaving an invisible string attaching him to her.

Emma stopped abruptly in front of her hotel. "This is me." Smiling, she peeled off his jacket, holding it out to him.

Sean took the jacket from her, placing it over his arm. "It was a real pleasure meeting you." He reached for the glass door, holding it open. "Here... I'll walk you to your room."

"Okay..." She brushed passed him, leading the way.

He gulped. His throat was suddenly raw as the two walked side by side. All he wanted to do was pull her close in an embrace, helping her forget about the other guy. His went mind blank, making it difficult for him to form a coherent thought.

"This is me." Emma stopped in front of her room. She reached into her purse, digging out her hotel room keycard. "Thanks for a great night... and for all your help with my skiing debacle." She moved to put it in the door.

He didn't want her to go, didn't want this to be their last interaction, even though tomorrow she would be gone.

Sean cleared his throat. "Can... I call you sometime?" He stumbled over the words. Emma made him feel like a teenager all over again. Unsure of himself in the presence of a beautiful woman.

Her eyes widened for a moment, then a smile crept across her face. "Sure. Why not?"

Sean grinned. "Perfect. I've got your number. I'll call you sometime. You have a nice trip back."

The man had no master plan, no divinely directed course. He simply liked Emma and he wanted to make her smile. Maybe it was his overly eager hero complex.

Emma pushed open her door, waving as she slipped inside.

Chapter Five

The drive back home was uneventful. Melanie slept in the passenger seat as the soft sounds of the radio filled the car, coupled with her snoring. Emma dreaded returning to her empty apartment. Being on vacation was entirely different from facing the reality of her *real* life.

Pine trees covered in heavy snow lined the narrow road, whipping past her and melting into a sea of white in her rear-view mirror. She wondered if Jake regretted his decision, and if he would come back. He told her he never loved her. Words she found impossible to forget, but secretly she still wished things wouldn't work out for him and his old flame. She wanted him to come crawling back, begging for forgiveness. Shaking her head, she pushed out the dangerous trail of thoughts she refused to travel down. No more dwelling in the past.

With each twist and turn on the road, slowly the events of the night before with Sean replayed in her mind. She sighed, tapping her fingers on the steering wheel. He was cute, attentive, and kind. The man had surprised her, especially when he shared about his mom leaving. Something told her it wasn't something he shared often with others. His easygoing personality seemed to mask the trauma of his childhood.

On the floor of the back seat sat her packed to-go box. The thought of eating it tonight brought a smile to her face. Sean certainly knew how to date. How was a guy like him single? It blew her mind. The man was the total package. If things were different, if she wasn't broken, she imagined she would jump at the chance to date him. Granted, Emma knew Sean had taken her out on a date due to pity. He felt sorry for her, nothing more.

After the quick hour drive, Emma pulled into the driveway of her parents' home. She lived in an apartment about five minutes away.

Anxious, her hands were jittery, like she had downed a few red bulls. She reached over, lightly shaking Melanie awake. "Mom, wake up. We're here."

Melanie's eyes fluttered opened, and she rubbed them until she fully woke up. "Already? I guess I slept the entire way home." She reached over and unbuckled her seat belt. Then she opened her door.

Emma went around to the back, popping open the trunk. She pulled out her mom's rolling suitcase and set it down on the driveway. Closing the trunk, she shoved her shaky hands into her pockets. The last thing she needed was for her mom to worry and insist on accompanying her to her apartment. This was something she needed to face on her own. She hugged Melanie.

"Thanks for everything, Mom. I'm going to be okay. Promise."

Melanie scanned her face. "Are you sure?"

Though she would be facing an empty apartment, alone, she didn't want to face it with anyone else. Did she fully plan on wallowing in self-pity? Yes, but she wanted to do so in private. There was a pint of ice cream at the bottom of her freezer calling her name. She planned on eating the entire thing, guilt free, while she cried. At least she had a plan.

"I'll be fine." She looked away, not wanting her mom to see the emotions bubbling up her. "I've got to face my demons at some point. I can't run away forever."

"You take care of yourself. Call me if you need anything." Melanie squeezed her shoulder. "You're going to be fine. I know it. Only good things to come."

Emma fluttered her glance back to Melanie. "They certainly can only go up from here."

Her sarcasm wasn't lost on Melanie. She raised an eyebrow. "Do you want to come in and say hi to your dad?"

Inwardly, she groaned. If she saw her dad and his sad eyes, the waterworks would start. "No. I'll see you both next Sunday for dinner."

Emma walked around to her car door, sliding into the driver's seat. All she wanted to do was peel out of their driveway before being forced to answer any more questions. She clearly wasn't okay. Nor would she be anytime soon, but no amount of coddling by her parents was going to help.

"See you next week." Melanie rolled her suitcase to the front door.

Emma closed her door, and backed out of the driveway. Once the view of her childhood home was no longer in the reflection of her rearview mirror, she lost it. Completely lost it. The tears flowed down her cheeks, and she pulled her car over to the side of the road. Her body shook in convulsions.

"Why?" she screamed to the empty car, pounding on the steering wheel.

The entire week she had been forced to put on a brave face, mostly to reassure all those in her life that she could handle it. There was nothing she couldn't handle, even a broken heart. She wanted others to believe she had a resounding inner strength. Lies, all lies. No more. Emma didn't feel strong. Fragile was the more accurate description. Like one more wrong thing and all the carefully glued together pieces of her would shatter.

Finally, her shoulders stopped shaking. She wiped tears from her face with the back of her hand. *Inhale. Exhale. Breathe.* With the quick flip of her wrist, she started the car, pulling carefully back onto the road to her apartment.

When her apartment came into view, her stomach sunk like a treasure trunk going overboard. Pulling into her spot, she parked, then grabbed her bags out of the car.

Fiddling with her keys, she stared at her ghostly image in the elevator mirrors.

The elevator dinged at her floor, and the doors opened. Steps heavy, she made her way to her door. Lingering, she mustered up courage and slid the key into the lock, pushing open the door. A quick sweep of the room revealed what she had anticipated. Just like she thought, Jake had moved out the few things he had brought over the week before.

Her eyes landed on the kitchen table. In the middle was her spare key, along with a sheet of paper. A fresh batch of tears cascaded down her cheeks as she walked over, picking up the note.

For a second, she imagined it was a note filled with regret and remorse. A note confessing he had been wrong and wanted to try again, but it wasn't that kind of note. It simply read, *I'm sorry. Jake.* Her heart clenched. It was the final nail in the coffin. Any hope she had held onto of their reconciliation was gone.

Emma crumbled the note in her hands and threw it forcefully against the wall of her living room. "This can't be happening," she shrieked, border lining a full, totally losing it scream. Her voice rang back and forth in the empty space, making her temples throb.

Rage filled her body, like she had received a steroid shot

and was ready for some WWF wrestling. She picked up the spare key, gripping it so hard it pierced her skin. Palm stinging, she yelped in pain as drops of blood dripped down her hand.

In one swift movement, she swiped the spare key into the junk drawer. Next, she grabbed a paper towel, pressing it against her bleeding palm. With nothing left to do, she slinked her body down the entire length of her refrigerator, sitting against the cold, hard stainless-steel metal. Plunging her head forward into her hands, she cried some more.

In the midst of her pity party, her phone binged, interrupting her dark thoughts. Reluctantly, she pulled her phone out of her pocket and glanced at down at the screen.

Her heart skipped a beat. The heavy darkness engulfing her lifted for a moment.

Sean: I hope you made it home okay.

His message washed over her like high tide, taking away part of the ache with it.

The words weren't anything profound, but they were from Sean. He cared. With phone in hand, she mulled over how to respond. The steady rise of her heartbeat warmed her entire body, making her stomach swim.

Her finger flew over her phone screen.

Emma: Yep. Made it home a little while ago. I'm just about to microwave my extra dinner from last night.

Wiping away the last stray tears, she catapulted herself to stand. Emma grabbed the to-go box, popping it into the microwave to warm it up. The thought of the warm fettucine made the situation seem less bleak. Though her life was a total mess, at least she had a plate of warm pasta to fill her belly. A sure cure for all ills.

Her phone binged again, and she quickly grabbed it off the kitchen counter.

Sean: Great. Want me to call you so you don't have to eat alone?

Emma wistfully sighed. Who was this guy, Sean? Swooping in right when she needed someone the most. He's only a friend, remember? A nice guy. Nothing more. Even that argument quickly dissipated. She liked Sean. Like really liked him. Though the whole thing had additional heartbreak written all over it, and against her better judgement, she found herself typing back enthusiastically.

Emma: Please do.

Her phone rang within minutes. Emma tucked her hair behind her ears and exhaled. Maybe the pint of ice cream would stay buried at the bottom of her freezer after all? Nah, who was she kidding? She planned on eating it, too.

* * *

Sean popped his to-go box into his microwave. His Saturday had been uneventful. As a vet, he was always on call. Over the years he learned, the weekends when he wanted to keep busy, his phone remained silent. The weekends he had something planned, he found himself called in and plans were broken. Today was no different.

With his extra time, his mind kept wandering back to Emma. Emma and her mysterious, unexplainable appeal. A woman who made him break his guarded boundaries. His rules of keeping things causal were quickly thrown out like the trash.

The man was in his late thirties, and he had managed to never date a woman for more than a year. Within those relationships, all short and shallow, he never once managed to tell anyone of them about his mom abandoning him. Then Emma came waltzing into his life, and he wanted more than anything to make her smile. To ease her heart break. To divulge more of himself because he trusted her. Why? He'd love to know.

The ding of his microwave interrupted his thoughts.

Grabbing his food out of the microwave, he settled down at his kitchen table. One which only had room for two, because his apartment above his vet clinic was pocket size. His kitchen was minuscule. A place only fit for a bachelor. Though he and his dad had lived in it his whole life, his mom had complained nonstop about its size his entire childhood.

Then, a few years ago, his dad wanted to retire. Sean bought his dad out of his practice, which meant the little apartment he grew up in, along with the vet clinic, now belonged to him. With the money his dad received for the practice, he bought an RV to drive across country, visiting rustic places. A man of simple desires, the RV life fit him like a glove. Every few months, his dad came back to visit. There was a nice, convenient place in the back parking lot, behind the clinic, where he parked his RV.

For a long time, he had wondered if his dad would ever get remarried. Years passed by and his dad showed zero interest in dating anyone. His scars of abandonment went even deeper than his own. Instead, he preferred traveling the world alone without the distraction or bother of a woman. So, when Sean remained unmarried far past the years of acceptable bachelorhood, his dad didn't even bat an eye. Never once had he asked why. Both knew why. It was always there, right below the surface. A wound which had never healed properly.

He placed his phone down on top of the table and called Emma. He hit the speakerphone button so he could eat and talk at the same time.

Emma picked on the second ring. "Sean." Her voice sounded breathless. "How's your day going?"

"It's good to hear your voice." He smiled. The familiar flutter in his stomach back. "Did you already start eating?" Sean used his fork to pierce a piece of pasta, shoving it into his mouth.

"I'm sitting down as we speak." A beat of silence followed as they both chewed. "Just as good as last night."

"I know, right? Only the best for you." He cringed at his lame attempt at flirting. Who was he? The man sounded like a babbling idiot. A splash of heat hit his cheeks. Clearing his throat, he willed himself to settle down.

Emma chuckled. The sound loosening the tightness in his chest.

"I do deserve the best," teased Emma.

"I completely agree." Sean popped open his soda and took a swig.

"At least we can say we agree on something," added Emma.

Sean smirked. The loneliness he had been experiencing since the weekend started, dissipated. "How was your drive home?"

"Not bad. It took about an hour. My mom slept the entire way."

"I think it's in a parent's DNA to fall asleep in the car. My dad can't make it five minutes in the passenger seat before he drifts off."

Emma exclaimed, "Not yours, too!" He could hear the grin in her voice.

His heart melted. Sean found purpose in making Emma happy again.

A pause followed. "Do I dare asked about the state of your apartment when you returned? I'm sure it wasn't easy."

The silence on the other end was deafening. He was pushing his own deliberately engineered line. Lines begone, he wanted to know how he could help Emma.

"It's awful. You've no idea." Her voice was decidedly less animated. "The worse part was he left a note on my kitchen counter with his key." She paused, exhaling. "Two words. The note had two words. That's all he wrote. I'm sorry... Like that's somehow supposed to magically make all the pain he caused go away."

"Yikes." He recoiled. "That's cold. Real cold. I'm sorry."

He took another sip of his soda, pondering what he would've done in that situation. The thought was halted in its tracks. Sean never planned on proposing to anyone, and though he was no love expert, he believed if you almost married a person, they deserved more than a simple note saying sorry.

Emma's response interrupted his thoughts. "I can't believe it. Anything would've been better than that. No note. I could've handled, but the fact he took the time to write that and nothing else, means he isn't sorry at all. Well, I don't forgive him. I just don't." Her voice shook as if she was fighting back tears.

Heart clenched, he wished for nothing more than to be with her, to wrap his arm around her in an embrace. *Focus brain. Stay in the moment.* This was his cue to lighten the mood. "Ahh. Give it time. You don't seem like the type who doesn't forgive a person. If anything, I bet you're quite the opposite. Eventually, you'll be thanking him. Someday, you'll be glad you didn't marry him."

Sean stood from the table, grabbing some napkins to wipe his face.

"You're probably right. Eventually, I know I won't hate his very existence. I might even wish him well."

Sean sat back down and leaned forward in his chair. Taking the phone off speakerphone, he held it to his ear. "He did you a favor." He spoke slowly, giving the proper emphasis to each word. "Repeat that to yourself whenever you start to question the whole thing."

"That's what everyone keeps saying." Emma wailed, sniffling. "I wished I hadn't loved him. This whole thing would be a lot easier."

"This will get easier. I promise." He grabbed his empty to-go box, throwing it into his trash can. "Trust me. You're at the worse part. It can only go up from here."

She cried some more. "How would you know?" Sean heard her blow her nose before continuing. "Have you ever been in engaged and had it broken off?"

Engaged. The single word rattled him, sending a shiver down his spine. No, he hadn't been engaged, nor would he ever be. The world had two camps: those who married, and those who didn't. He was firmly planted in the "never marry" camp. Marriage was a miserable institution. One he refused to buy into.

"Nah. I've never been engaged or married." He plopped himself down on his old worn-out brown leather sofa, getting comfortable. "Emma, you need to think rationally. Who wants to marry someone who doesn't want them?"

"Nobody." Her voice sounded deflated, like the last bit of air was being released from a balloon.

"Cheer up. The universe is working overtime right now." Sean laid back on the sofa, adjusting a pillow behind his head. "It's working to bring you your perfect match... It isn't Jake. Trust me."

"You really think so?" asked Emma.

"I do." He placed his hand behind his head, crossing his ankles. "Change of subject. Time to talk about something which will lighten your mood. I've personally taken on the job full heartedly." Sean enjoyed talking with Emma more than any other woman he had met.

Emma chuckled. "What do you suggest?"

"What was the last thing you watched?" The question popped into his head like he was talking to an old friend. A person he had known forever and not like two days.

"Have you seen the new documentary about the Arctic?" Her voice rose an octave.

He sat straight up. This might be his dream girl. "Have I? I live for those." He grabbed his remote off the coffee table and turned on the T.V. Muting it as not to disturb their conversation, he scrolled through the selection of shows.

"I figured you did," said Emma, her voice upbeat, "being a vet and all."

"You've guessed right."

They talked about their mutual love of animal documentaries. It wasn't anything earth shattering, but for once in his life, he imagined what it would be like to have someone. A person to snuggle up on the couch with after a long day and unwind together with an animal documentary. Not some unrealistic fantasy. Fantasies a person conjured up and led them to a life of disappointment. No. An obtainable reality, with Emma in it. The idea was oddly comforting.

As the hour got late, Sean yawned.

"I heard that." Emma acknowledged on the other end of the phone.

Without warning, Sean yawned again. "You've caught me. I guess I'm not used to staying up this late."

She sighed. "Either am I. I guess it's time we say goodbye."

Sean ended the call and clicked off his phone, settling his body comfortably into the sofa cushions.

His body hadn't been this relaxed in a long time, and he had no plans to ruin it by moving to his bed. Instead, he grabbed the blanket sprawled haphazardly across the back of the sofa, wrapping it around himself. Snuggling deeper into the sofa, he contently drifted off to sleep. Dreaming of only one woman, Emma.

Chapter Six

Monday morning greeted Emma bright and early. The buzzing of her alarm clock awoke her from her peaceful slumber. She groaned as she pulled back the covers. The chill of winter hit her skin, making her shiver. Gingerly, and only half awake, she made her way to the bathroom.

Today was her first day back at teaching. The dreaded day where the thought of facing her co-workers made her blood run cold. The many questions she would face made her want to crawl back into bed and call in sick.

"You can do this." She tried her best to sound strong and resilient as she spoke to her reflection in the mirror.

Slapping her hand on top of the cool marble vanity, the stone was slick under her fingertips. She gripped the end tightly, making her knuckles turn white. "You've got this." She nodded enthusiastically, willing herself to believe in her inner strength.

She probably didn't, but she had no choice but to face her demons. Taking a deep breath, she left the comfort of the bathroom and went to get ready for work.

When she pulled into the school parking lot, she spotted

Anna, a fellow teacher and friend, and waved through the window.

Anna pivoted and waited for Emma to get out of her car. "It's good to see you!"

"Hi, Anna." Emma reached across the middle console, grabbing her purse off the passenger seat. "Just a second. Let me grab my stuff, and I'll walk in with you." She gathered her things and got out of the car. She swung her purse over her shoulder, closing the door.

Anna pulled her in for a hug. "How's everything going?" she asked slowly, her eyes darting across her, searching for an indication of Emma's emotions.

Emma raised an eyebrow. "How do you think I'm doing?"

The two started walking from the parking lot into the school. The school was a single building which had different hallways, all breaking off from the main office. Each wing held the classrooms of a specific grade. Anna and Emma taught third grade, so their classrooms were right next to each other. Their friendship had been a fast one in the making. Both started teaching at the same time and enjoyed working with one another. They often ate lunch together and exchanged war stories of being in a classroom full of kids all day.

Anna lowered her voice as they entered the main office of the school. "Horrible," she added.

Emma stripped off her thick winter coat to keep from sweating. The heat was cranked up, and the school was warm and cozy. A stark contrast to the bitter air outside.

"You are correct, my dear."

Anna bit down on her bottom lip. "Do I even ask how the ski trip with your mom went?"

Emma laughed sarcastically. "It was a dream come true to go on a honeymoon trip with my *mom*."

"I bet. A real trip to paradise." Anna gave Emma's shoulder a slight squeeze. "Sorry I asked."

"It shows you care," added Emma in front of her classroom. She dug around in her purse for her keys, locating them to unlock the door. "The only bright spot in the entire week was this guy, Sean, who helped save me while I was skiing. I mean, he didn't save me, but he waited until the ski patrol came."

Anna clapped her hands together, eyes as wide as an owl. "What? You're kidding?"

Emma pushed open her door, then she turned back to face her. "Nope. True story."

"Why didn't you lead with that?" Anna raised an eyebrow. "I'm all ears."

A fellow teacher passed them in the hallway, so Emma smiled and waved before she replied. "I was wondering if I should say anything or not. It's probably nothing. But he asked me out to dinner, and we hit it off. We have been talking every night over the phone since I've returned."

Anna's jaw dropped. "What?!" She made an expression with her hands showing her mind was blown. "My mind is reeling." She glanced down at her watch and sighed. "I wished we had time for you to tell me the entire story. Lunch?"

For the first time, the weight of facing the day and seeing all her co-workers was lifted. Emma smiled. "You bet. I'll tell you about the whole story at lunch."

The morning flew by. All her students were excited to tell her all about their winter break. None seemed overly phased when she briefly explained that she didn't get married. She dodged any questions from them by announcing their art project for the day. Without missing a beat, she passed out the supplies, and the entire subject of her failed wedding didn't resurface again.

By lunch, she needed a break and breathed a sigh of relief for the respite. Emma loved teaching, but every year after winter break, she always found it hard to get back in the groove of the constant demands. By the end of the week, she would be back in the full swing of things.

Within seconds of the bell ringing, grinning, Anna entered Emma's classroom with her lunch in hand. She slid into one of the seats at the back table. "I've been dying to hear all about Mr. Wonderful who saved you," she said in a sing-song voice.

Emma grabbed her lunch out of her mini fridge and took a seat. "I'm glad I've got something to share besides being dumped." She popped open her soda and took a swig before continuing. "The guy I met, Sean, is a local veterinarian in Bluebird. A few days into the trip, I went flying down the mountain way too fast and slammed into a tree well. I was stuck, and the ski patrol had to dig me out. Sean saw the entire thing and came over to make sure I wasn't injured. After the ambulance took me to the hospital, he stayed with my mom until they confirmed I was going to be fine."

Anna leaned forward, cradling her chin. "Incredible. Why do some people have all the luck?" She sighed, then waved her hand. "I'm kidding, but I like this guy already. I need more details. So, he stayed with your mom. Then what? You need to get to the part where he asked you out." She took a bite from her turkey sandwich.

Wistfully, Emma sighed as she remembered dinner with Sean. She shook her head, glancing back at Anna. "After I checked out of the hospital, my mom insisted we swing by his veterinarian clinic to thank him. When I visited with a few bakery items, he asked me out. On the date, we just hit it off." She opened her yogurt, plunging her spoon into it. She took a bite.

Emma was forever grateful that Sean found a way to help her forget about Jake. On an impossibly hard day of returning to her empty apartment, he lifted her spirit. Talking over the phone every night since then had only deepened the connection. She couldn't ever remember sharing with a guy all the things she divulged to him and only in the span of a week. Sean was a great listener. Never interrupted, but instead, he listened like every word she said mattered.

Anna reached across the table, grabbing Emma's hand. "I'm so happy for you." She paused, then continued. "Tell me... Does this guy have a brother?"

Emma raised an eyebrow, confused. "What?"

"Does he have a brother?" Anna repeated as she leaned back in her chair. "If he has one, I want to date him. Good looks and manners usually run in families."

Emma laughed. "Sorry. No brothers. He's an only child like me."

"That's too bad." Anna exhaled. "It was worth asking."

Emma grinned. "Don't worry, I'm sure someday soon Ben will propose." Anna had been dating Ben for as long as she could remember, but she was starting to get anxious. Wondering if it was time for her to cut Ben loose and move on. "Then you'll be the one walking down the aisle. I know it."

Anna rolled her eyes. "I keep dropping hints, but he doesn't seem to be taking the bait." She took another bite of her sandwich and opened her bag of chips.

"Whatever." Emma waved off her comment. "He'll propose soon. He's crazy about you."

"I do worry." Anna stopped eating, glancing at Emma. "What if I'm wasting my time on a guy who'll never marry me?"

Emma stirred her yogurt, wondering how to respond. Anna had revealed numerous times that she wanted nothing more than to marry Ben. Emma wasn't one who could give any sound advice in the romance department. Look at her. She had wasted years of her life on Jake. In hindsight, she wished she had walked away from him long before she had ever become engaged. But Emma had seen Ben and Anna together, they were perfect for one another.

Emma cleared her throat. "You aren't." She gave a reassuring smile, trying to help soothe the anxiety in Anna's heart. "He practically told me the last time we all hung out. He wants to marry you. It's coming. Don't worry."

"Really?" Anna's face brightened at the revelation.

Emma nodded. "Yep. Promise."

Their half hour lunch neared the end, so Anna gathered her trash and threw it away. She walked toward the door to leave. Looking over her shoulder she said, "Keep me updated on things with Sean. I have a good feeling about this guy."

"You do?" Emma asked, searching for a bit of reassurance.

Pivoting at the threshold, she glanced at Emma with a bright grin. "I do. I need to go make some copies before the bell rings, but I think you're going to be just fine."

Glancing up at the clock above her whiteboard, Emma saw she only had a few minutes before lunch was over. She gathered her trash and tossed it. Slipping into her desk chair, she glanced out the window. The playground was full of kids playing together. The sight warmed her soul. She smiled as the sounds of kids laughing and squealing became noticeable once again. Though the last few weeks had been a doozy, Sean was giving her a glimmer of hope. Perhaps even her new beginning... one could dream.

"Peanut should feel better real soon." Sean ripped off the written prescription from his pad and handed it to Mr. Meek.

Mr. Meek took the prescription paper from him, glancing down. "This is all Peanut needs?" He skeptically looked over at him.

"Yes. It's only a simple case of tapeworms. Peanut should

feel fit as a fiddle in a few days." Sean made an additional note on the cat's chart.

"I guess I'll take your word for it. Thanks Doc." Mr. Meek lifted his cat and placed him in his crate, locking Peanut inside.

"I'll walk you out." Sean opened the door to the exam room, letting Mr. Meek pass through first, and he followed behind him to the front lobby. Mr. Meek slipped out the door into the cold wintery day.

Smiling, Sean walked toward the front window, watching as Mr. Meek headed a few doors down to the pharmacy. His spirit was light. With Emma in his life, even the darkest, dreariest day seemed worth living.

"It's certainly a beautiful day out." He pivoted back, making eye contact with Julie. "I love all this snow."

Julie glanced over at him from her desk. "What's up with you? A beautiful day... What are you smoking?" She eyed him suspiciously. "It's a total mess out there. Took me an extra ten minutes to get here because the roads are one slushy mess. I thought I was going to die trying to make it on time. Besides, you of all people hate snowstorms."

It was freezing cold outside. The roads were horrible. Currently, everything looked white and fresh, but in a few hours, the winter wonderland would be one dirty mess. A mixture of rock salt, mud, and snow. The bad roads were sure to cause delays with his clients. Though Mr. Meek had managed to arrive on time for his appointment, that was most likely a fluke. His other clients would probably arrive late and out of order all day long.

None of it phased him. Sean was happy. His late-night conversations with Emma over the last several days brought a smile to his face. They had talked about everything. From random stories from high school and college to their favorite food and restaurants. They never failed to find something new to discuss. Never in his life had he experienced anything like it. Talking to Emma was easy and natural.

He shrugged. "Nothing is up with me." Smiling, he pulled his glance from Julie back to the front window. "Can't a guy enjoy a snowy day?"

"No... you're such a liar." Julie leaned back in her chair, crossing her arms. "Something is up with you. You're in too good of a mood for a snowy day." She tapped her bottom lip with her pointer finger. "It's something to do with that woman who came into the clinic. The one you asked out. Isn't it?"

He pulled his eyes from the window and walked back toward Julie. "Emma?"

Julie snapped and pointed. "That's her name. Emma. Did the date go that well?" Her eyes widened.

Sean laughed. "Is it that obvious?"

Julie had watched him date practically every woman in Bluebird, but she had never made a comment like this before. It piqued his interest. The fact Julie recognized a change in him was a first.

"Obvious?" Julie laughed. Rising, she stepped over to the shelves which lined the wall behind her desk, pulling the needed files for the rest of the morning appointments. "I think Emma is different. I can feel it. Your whole temperament has changed. So, watch out. You might not be a bachelor much longer."

She handed him the file for his next client. Taking it, he forced a laugh. "Let's not get ahead of ourselves," added Sean.

Julie settled back into her chair. "I don't think I am." Her statement lingered in the air before she began typing.

Something stirred within Sean, a longing to finally be part of a couple. In the past, any thought of commitment made his blood run cold, forcing him toward the nearest exit. He waited for the pit in his stomach to form from Julie's comments, but it didn't come.

The bell on the door sounded, and he glanced up. His next client arrived on time. Nothing was going to dampen his good mood.

"Welcome, Mr. Jones." Sean stepped toward him, holding out his extended hand. Mr. Jones shook it. "I'm glad you made it okay with the roads being a mess. Bring Jupiter back, and I'll see her right away." Sean motioned for Mr. Jones to follow him to the exam room.

The day was busy and hectic. A steady stream of clients trickled in. Some on time, others not, but nothing he couldn't handle. Sean settled into his office for lunch. Pulling out his sandwich, chips, and soda, he began to eat. Removing his phone from his pocket, he wanted to turn on a podcast while he ate but there was a missed call from his dad.

Sean turned the phone to speaker and hit play. "Sean...I know it's been a while since I've called. Sorry. My cell reception has been spotty. But I'll be back in town tomorrow and I want to talk... I've some news to share." A long pause. His message continued. "Okay... I'll see you tomorrow night. We'll talk then. I should be there around 6."

The message ended. Sean played it again. His dad was withholding something from him. He could hear it in his voice. His stomach plummeted like he was on one of those weird elevators drop rides. Bile burned his throat. Sean grabbed his soda and forced a swig to wash the burning battery acid taste back down. Something was wrong. Terribly, terribly wrong. Sweat glistened his brow. His mind ran rampant with various worse case scenarios. He couldn't lose his dad. He was all he had. The thought terrified him.

Swiveling in his chair, his eyes landed on the mess outside his office window. The crisp snow which had blanketed the earth earlier in the morning was replaced with a dirty, wet mess. His jaw clenched. His good mood vanished as he worried about his dad's call.

Julie knocked lightly on his office door, interrupting his thoughts. "I received a call from a farm out in Hardwick." She eyed him. "They're in desperate need of someone to look at one of their horses. You only have two appointments this afternoon. Do you want me to cancel them and reschedule them for tomorrow? They probably wouldn't mind, since the roads are still horrible."

Hardwick was only fifteen minutes from Emma. Whoa, where did that come from? The message from his dad evaporated into thin air. Man, he was in deep. Maybe Emma would be willing to meet him for dinner after his appointment? Worth a try. And just like that, his good mood was back.

A smile crept across his face. "Sure. Let them know I'm on my way."

Julie eyed him suspiciously. "You seem awful chipper for a guy who has to drive across the state in bad weather to treat a horse in sub-freezing temperature." She put her hand on her hip. "What gives?"

Sean leaned back in his chair, clearing his throat. "Fine. If you must know, Emma lives fifteen minutes from there. I thought I might see if she is available to meet for dinner after the appointment."

Julie smirked. "Just like I thought." She laughed, walking away to cancel his afternoon appointments. "I called it." She yelled over her shoulder.

Julie's comment didn't rattle him, instead with a second wind, he grabbed his phone and typed out a text to Emma.

Sean: I've got a last-minute appointment for a horse in Hardwick this afternoon. Would you want to meet me for dinner around 7?

As he waited for her to respond, he gathered his medical

bag and other items he knew he needed for his visit. His phone dinged, and he quickly swiped it off his desk.

Emma: That works. Tell me where and I'll be there.

He exhaled. Rapidly, he replied with the address of a restaurant he knew in the area. Sean continued to ready his medical bag.

His phone binged. **I'll see you tonight at 7.**

Julie was probably right. Emma had him hook, line, and sinker. The idea simmered below the surface. He waited for the panic to come, for him to run for the hills. Instead, he found himself excited at the idea of seeing Emma so soon. Especially since their late-night conversations still had him reeling, dreaming about kissing her. With one last scan of his office, he grabbed his jacket off the coat rack and headed out the door.

Chapter Seven

After pulling into the parking lot, Emma double checked the address of the restaurant on her phone. The lot was only partially full, most likely due to the bad weather. The roads were awful. She had white knuckled it the entire drive, but nothing was going to ruin her evening. Sean, with his piercing baby blues and wind-swept hair, had invited her to dinner. He was a distraction, she knew that, but she welcomed the reprieve. A guy to help her forget Jake. Even with that knowledge, she couldn't deny how easy he was to talk to or how he made her feel understood.

Glancing down at her watch, she tapped her fingers on the steering wheel. She had arrived a little early. Her mind wandered to their phone conversations. She wondered what it would be like to kiss Sean. If they could be more than friends. Off she went, letting her mind wander to places it wasn't ready to go. This time she needed to be cautious, take her time to fully mend her broken heart. All of that was the logical thing to do, but she had never been logical when it came to men.

In the visor mirror, she double checked her hair and makeup. Luckily, she had time after work to freshen up a bit before driving to meet him. She pouted at her reflection, wrinkles spanning between her eyes and laugh lines dangerously close to becoming permanent. Without a thought, she rubbed her hands over the uneven skin in an attempt to smooth out the lines. It was fruitless. She slammed the mirror closed. Sean knew what she looked like, and there was zero use in getting all worked up over it. He either liked what he saw, or he didn't. Squaring her shoulders, she slipped out of her car.

Entering the restaurant, she made a quick scan for Sean. Not spotting him, she approached the host in a black and white uniform with her hair tied tightly back in a bun, standing behind a wood podium. "Welcome to Morton's Steakhouse. How may I help you?" Her voice was overly cheerful, calming her nerves.

"Hi. I..." Emma glanced around her. "I think I've arrived before my date. Do you have a reservation under Sean for two by chance? Can you see if he has checked in?"

"No problem. Let me see..." The host glanced down at the tablet with the reservations. She scrolled through the list of names, while Emma leaned over the podium, scanning for Sean's name as well.

Emma spotted his name, pointing. "It's right there."

The host looked up, smiling. "Great. He hasn't checked in yet. Do you want to wait in the lobby, or do you want to be taken back to your table?"

Emma hesitated, scanning her watch. It was already five past seven. She wondered what was best. "My date should be here any minute..." She bit down on her bottom lip. "Is it okay if I'm seated? Then could you let Sean know where I am when he arrives?"

"Absolutely. Not a problem." She grabbed two menus off the stack behind the podium on a credenza, then motioned for Emma to follow. "Right this way." She glanced over her shoulder as they wandered through the restaurant. "Since it's a date, I'll seat you in my favorite booth."

Emma smiled. "Thanks. That's very nice of you. I appreciate it."

The host stopped in front of a booth nicely situated toward the back of the restaurant. The table was dressed in white linens, sparkly silverware, and a candle centerpiece. A more intimate place than some of the tables near the waiting area.

"Thanks." Emma slid into the booth, taking the menu from the host. "This is a lovely spot."

The host winked. "Anything for love. I hope you two have a nice dinner."

Her cheeks burned with a flash of heat. All the extra attention from the host made her acutely aware of what might be riding on tonight. Emma opened the menu, scanning the selection of items. A mix of steak and chicken along with a few fish choices. The place was way nicer place than how she normally dined on her measly teacher's salary. Anxiety coursed through her body as her stomach did somersaults. With no sign of Sean, she glanced at her watch. He was ten minutes late and hadn't called or texted. A sign which meant he was en route?

Her leg bounced and bobbed under the table. Surely, he wouldn't stand her up? Sean was the one to initiate the date. She brushed away the thought, willing her quickened pulse to slow back down. Heat rose inch by inch up her neck, slathering it in red. Her signature look when she was anxious. In an attempt to cool herself down, she lightly fanned her face with her hand. *Calm down. Calm down. Calm. Down.* Sean was one of the good ones. A far cry from Jake. He isn't ditching you, too.

After a few more minutes, the server stopped by the table.

She smiled awkwardly over the top of her menu. The man held a bottle of wine in his hands.

"Good evening. I'm John, and I'll be your server this evening. Are you still waiting for someone?"

She shifted in the booth, peering back up to the front of the restaurant. "My date isn't here yet." She gnawed on her bottom lip. "I'm sorry. He was supposed to be here fifteen minutes ago, but he must be caught up in this weather. The roads were bad for me."

Without missing a beat, the server responded, "Not a problem. I'll send over a bread basket while you wait. Can I get you something to drink?"

Shifting in her seat, she finally met the server's eyes. "Sure." She threw her hands up in defeat and ordered something to drink.

Once the server left, Emma pulled out her phone, typing rapidly.

Emma: Are you okay? I'm already seated and hope you didn't get stuck somewhere on the bad roads. Let me know if you are still coming. She hit send and slid her phone back into her purse. Nervously, she tapped the top of the table.

Was she getting stood up? Nonsense. Emma shook her head, reminding herself he asked her out. It wasn't the other way around. Sean had shown interest. He was the one who called her on the day she returned home. All the initiation had been from him. A man didn't ask a woman out and then not show.

Emma thanked a server who dropped off a basket of bread, her mind still a muddled mess. She willed herself to not spiral and not jump to any conclusions. Then she made the mistake of checking her watch, and her tough exterior crumbled. Twenty-two minutes and counting. Where was he? Everyone knew it was common courtesy to text a person and let them know you were running late. Hopefully, he hadn't been involved in an accident. A sad, but reasonable explanation.

Grabbing a piece of the warm bread, she spread butter across the top. It melted, seeping into the fluffy texture. One more time, she peered back at the front door. Nothing. She took a bite, chewing, not tasting a single morsel. After she finished off her piece, mindlessly, she reached and took another, eating a pound of bread as a distraction when the server brought her drink.

Emma forced a tight smile. "Thanks." Reverting eye contact, she took a sip to wash down the bread. "I hope my date is here soon. If not, I believe I might've been stood up." She rearranged her silverware.

"I'm sure he is on his way..." His expression told her otherwise. "The roads are still awful out there. I had a hard time getting here."

She mustered up the last remaining bit of optimism she had, though she didn't believe a word of what was coming out of her mouth. "You're right. It's probably that."

Wiping her hands down her thighs, Emma rubbed them back and forth. Thirty-one minutes and no sign of Sean.

He gave a curt nod. "I'll swing back by in a few minutes." He waved his hand. "You can have the table for as long as you need."

Emma replied, "Thanks." Her lips forming a tight, overly forced, smile.

Palms dripping with sweat, she pulled out her phone with shaky hands.

One last text.

Emma: I'm really worried. I'll wait a few more minutes, and then I'm leaving. Aggressively, she hit send, throwing it back into her purse. Her temples throbbing, she found it hard to concentrate on anything but how worthless she felt.

Emma was a complete fool. Throwing caution to the wind, jumping in feet first when she knew her judgement was impaired. Her heart was already unsteady. She wanted to believe Sean was different. A gentleman. A man who didn't bail on a commitment, but it turned out he was like all the rest of them. She drummed her fingers on top of the table. After five more minutes, she removed a twenty-dollar bill from her wallet and placed it on the table. Sliding out of the booth, she made her best award-winning act to appear undeterred from the whole evening. She pulled her shoulders back, walking all the way through the restaurant with her head held high.

As she exited the restaurant, the brutal piercing air hit her skin like daggers. Her reflexes heightened. She pulled her coat tighter around herself, anything to help block out the bone chilling wind. The darkness of night had fully set, and only the glow of the streetlamps lighted her way to the car. Why had she allowed Sean into her life? She wasn't ready to date. It was a rookie mistake. One she didn't plan on repeating. She heard the message from the universe loud and clear. It was time to invest in some cats.

As she approached her car, the sound of her name broke her dark thoughts. Emma squinted in the direction her name was being called, making out the shadowy outline of a man. His being became clearer as he came closer. Sean. Her heart recoiled. Anger seeped into her veins.

"Emma! Emma! I'm here!" Sean shouted as he made his way toward her.

For a moment, he lost his footing on the newly fallen snow, but managed to recover and not fall, continuing his way toward her a few yards away.

Exhaling, she edged closer to her car and clicked the unlock button. Emma opened the driver's side door and tossed her purse on the passenger seat. *Jump in and drive away. Do it. Do. It.*

Instead, her feet remained firmly planted on the slick concrete. The snow continued to fall around them. "You're too late!" Emma shouted back, emotion bubbling up her throat.

Soon, Sean was in front of her, breathless.

She blinked rapidly, pushing her crumbling exterior away. "You're too late," she repeated.

Emma took in the whole hunky view of him. Her pulse quickened as the mere image of him slowly thawed the chill in her chest. She hated herself for her weak resolve. Hated her neediness, her inability to demand more than what she was always given. One look at him and she was ready to forgive all.

"I know... I know." Sean leaned forward, putting his hands on his knees as he caught his breath.

He reached out, touching her on her forearm. Her skin awakened. His fingers warmed her through her jacket. She finally met his eyeline. His face full of remorse unsettled her, rocking her to her core, forcing her logic and reason to go out the window.

Emma jutted her chin. "You should've called. Or texted. Anything," her voice cracked, revealing how much she cared. Revealing her insecurities and how hard she had already fallen.

Sean's labored breathing subsided. "Emma... I'm so sorry." He looked weary. He reached and lightly placed his hands on her shoulders. "You must believe me. I didn't mean to stand you up."

Folding her arms protectively against her body, she forced herself to remain stoic. "You didn't even call or text. I don't buy it," said Emma with a clenched jaw.

In the past, she had brushed off all the red flags. Especially with Jake, but not this time. This time, she wasn't looking past the myriad of sins which were deal breakers.

Sean dropped his hands, shoving them into his pockets.

"Emma." His voice lower, more mellow. "Please hear me out. I'll explain..."

With them no longer touching, her mind cleared. "I'll listen. Please continue."

Sean ran his fingers through his hair. He opened his mouth to speak but then closed it. He exhaled, making his shoulders droop. "I...I" He stammered. "I was way out on this farm, and I didn't have any cell service. It took me longer than I thought to treat their horse. By the time I realized how late it was, I frantically left to come here. As I was driving down their single dirt road to exit their farm..." He paused, searching her face for understanding. Emma raised an eyebrow at him, and he stumbled on his next words. "Still couldn't use my phone, by the way. A huge tractor flipped over. Blocked my way out. I had to get out and help. I was forced to walk all the way back to the farm to get the owner."

"Why didn't you call me from the house?" She let out an exasperated breath, throwing her arms down at her sides.

He slinked even further into his coat, biting his bottom lip. "I left my phone in my car. When I arrived to call for help, I had no way to call you. I don't have your number memorized." Sean stepped closer, bridging the gap between them. His gaze landed squarely on her, making her heart hammer. "I tried calling the restaurant, but I kept getting put on hold. I'd never stand you up on purpose. Promise." He made a motion across his heart.

Emma tried her best to sort through Sean's story. As strange as it sounded, she believed him. She held up both of her hands.

"Let's say I believe you and that whole ridiculous story..." She raised an eyebrow. "How do you plan on making this up to me?"

Grinning, Sean placed his arm around her, and she leaned into the warmth his body radiated. Their closeness, making her insides molten lava. He tilted his head toward her. "It will start with a complete redo of dinner."

Emma nudged him with her elbow. "That's a given." She smirked. "That isn't going to cut it. What else?"

Sean pulled her even closer. Emma wrapped her arm around his waist, and she glanced up at him. A mischievous look crossed his face.

"I've got it." He laughed. "I'll take you skiing."

Emma slapped him on the arm. "Very funny. Quite the comedian. I'm serious." She fidgeted with a few loose strands of her hair. "You've better make this right. I'm still angry at you."

Reaching out, Sean slowly covered her fidgeting hand with his. Then he tucked the few loose strands of her hair behind her ear. He leaned in, whispering into her hair. "It's a surprise..." A tickle ran down her spine. "But trust me, it'll be worth the wait."

His gaze found hers. She heard three steady beats of her heart. Defenseless to his charm and good-looks, Emma gulped.

Her voice weak, she replied, "I think... I think you just don't have a plan. Am I right?"

Sean leaned in, inches from her lips. Close enough, his lips barely touched hers as an invisible thread of desire danced between them. He paused. "You'll have to wait and see." The words tickled her neck and goose bumps ran rampant down her back.

The scent of his cologne whirled around, flaring her nostrils. Drawing her in, she bathed in the sweetness of the aroma. For one bold beat, Emma refused to pull her glance away. Positive, she was seconds away from being kissed. By him. For the first time. Never in her life had she coveted something more. She swallowed.

"Fine. Have it your way." Her voice shook.

"I will," said Sean, the two words lingering, creating a crackling live wire between them.

He tightened his arm around her waist. All she heard was the thumping of her temples. The moment passed like an eternity until he slowly crossed the impalpable barrier which held them apart. His lips glided over hers. Her mind went blank. Wherever his lips traveled, they left a tingly trail. His thumb smoothed the curve of her jaw in a slow, circular motion. The steady beating of her heart picked up its pace with each sweep. Knees weak, she allowed him to support her. She tugged on his jacket, forcing their bodies closer, until they were hip to hip. Fully melting herself against him, his hand traveled to the small of her back, holding her upright. Her other hand plunged into his hair while her lips parted to his. She wanted to live there in that moment, kissing him, forever.

Eventually, he pulled away. Gasping for air, she waited for her heartrate to return to normal. The tension in her chest lessened with each pulse. She studied his face, wondering and hoping he had shared the same life-alternating moment she had. Their shared minty breath fluttered in the space between them. He took her face into both of his hands, locking eyes with hers. Then he kissed her lightly on the temple, his fingers brushing her hair out of the way. Her mind was spinning like she was on a carousel. She blinked rapidly, willing herself to find solid ground.

He whispered into her ear, "I've wanted to do that since the first day I met you."

Emma felt him smirk. She pulled away enough to glance up at him.

"You don't say?" she asked, finding it hard to hide her surprise.

"No lie. You're so beautiful," he said, giving each word added emphasis.

A single finger slowly traced her jaw. She closed her eyes and drank in the feeling of his touch.

"Thanks." She croaked. The words caught in her throat.

He grinned. "You're welcome... but you already knew that." Sean cleared his throat. "I just wanted you to hear it from me."

A tantalizing line of goosebumps rushed down her body. She tipped her mouth closer to his. Her eyes flickered up to meet his gaze. This time, she kissed him first.

Chapter Eight

Later the next day, Sean finished some paperwork for his client in the lobby of his clinic. He was on cloud nine all day, smiling and whistling to himself. The man couldn't remember a time when he had been happier. It was Emma. An unexpected but wonderful surprise.

On his last note, he signed and handed the completed file to Julie, who sat at reception. She took the file from him and agreed to enter the information before leaving.

Sean nodded, his gaze traveling to the window facing Main Street. The evening winter hours settled over them as the streetlamps flicked on. He wondered when his dad would arrive. He was expecting him any minute.

Julie finished typing and organized some files before grabbing her coat from the lobby.

"That's it for me, boss. I'll see you tomorrow," she told Sean. "What time is your dad getting into town?" She pushed her arms into her coat. "I was hoping to say hello before I left."

Sean pivoted toward her. "Honestly, I thought he would be here by now. He normally tries to avoid driving after dark. He told me he has some news to share." He stepped closer to the window, peering both ways for any indication of his dad's RV. Gnawing at his fingernails, he desperately wanted Julie to convince him it was nothing. "I've no idea what he wants to tell me. This whole thing is eating me alive."

She wrapped her scarf around her neck and put on her gloves, asking, "Did he say if it was good news or bad news?"

Sean shook his head. "Nope. He just left a brief message saying he would be here today to tell me."

Julie swung her purse over her shoulder. Lightly, she tapped her gloved pointer finger on her bottom lip. "I've got it!" Her eyes twinkled with mischievousness. A smirk slowly spread across her face. "He's met someone."

Met someone? The words felt like a quick kick to the gut. Had Julie lost her mind? Never. Not ever. If anything, he had learned full heartedly from his dad how women were not to be trusted. Avoid at all costs. Run far and fast from them, though he wasn't running anywhere from Emma. If anything, he was running straight into her arms, an obvious flaw to his thinking.

Sean forced a laugh. "Nice one, Julie. My dad hasn't met someone. The man has been single for who knows how long. Where would he possibly meet someone?" He cleared his throat, forcing himself to simmer down. "It's something else. I just wish I knew what."

With a wave of her finger, Julie continued. "You never know." She strode across the room to the front door, reminding Sean to tell his dad she said hello. He held the door open for her, and she stepped out onto the sidewalk.

He peered once more in both directions. No sign of his dad. Sean went back into the warmth of his clinic, then continued to his office. There were still files that needed to be updated, so he sat down at his desk and tried to finish up his work while he waited for his dad's arrival.

The day had been hectic, but he remembered the text he

had sent earlier to Emma, asking her out on a date. Sean fished out his phone from his pocket. A message was waiting for him. His heart swelled, when he read the words.

Emma: Sounds great. Looking forward to this weekend.

He exhaled, remembering the kiss from the other night. The one which made his head spin. He didn't even recognize himself anymore. A simple text message from her made him swoon.

He had invited her to go maple tapping, which was done every winter in Vermont. After some research on the internet, he found a beautiful and quaint maple tree farm equal distance from both of their homes.

It was Julie's idea. He had explained the whole fiasco of the night before, and she helped him plan the outing. She had convinced him it was equal parts fun, creative, and romantic. All his life he had lived here, and not once had he gone to see the maple trees. Look at him. A maple tapping, planner. Whoa, he was in deep.

His thoughts were interrupted by his dad, Thomas. His voice traveled down the hallway of his clinic. "Sean, are you back there?!" Thomas yelled.

Sean slipped his phone back into his pocket. "Yep, I'm back here!"

He stood up, heading out of his office into the hallway. His jaw dropped, halting in place like a deer in headlights. Thomas wasn't alone. A woman's fingers were intertwined with his. Sean blinked. He was at a loss for words. Thomas glanced at the woman, then back at Sean.

Sean walked slowly, like he was having an out-of-body experience, toward his dad.

"I... Ah... Dad... Who's this?" He glanced between the couple, stopping in front of them.

Thomas managed a meek smile. "This is Lisa."

The woman had curly brown hair and deep, dark eyes. His dad never dated. To Sean's recollection, he couldn't remember a time Thomas held hands with anyone. Not even his mom.

"Lisa?" Sean repeated, his voice cracking.

Thomas shuffled his feet, eyeing Sean. Lisa tightened her grip on Thomas's arm.

Temples pulsing, heart thumping, his throat became dry. Thomas didn't need to explain a thing, it was written all over the man's face. The man had gone off and fallen in love.

Thomas and Lisa glanced at each other. He narrowed his eyes at Sean, challenging him to act less than gracious.

Sean ignored his pointed look, plunging his fingers through his hair. His mind spinning a mile a minute.

"Who's Lisa?" Sean willed his voice and temper to remain steady.

Thomas smiled at Lisa. Lisa squeezed Thomas' hand, peering over at him with an oozing love that made Sean's stomach churn. He wanted to hurl.

Staring at Lisa, Thomas replied, "My wife." He turned his head back to Sean and grinned. "We eloped."

Dead silence. He swore he heard crickets.

Inside.

In the middle of winter.

The words lingered in the air. Sucking out every bit of oxygen in the universe. He found it hard to breath. His lips failed to form any words. His dad got married? Sean could handle his dad having a girlfriend, but not married to a woman who he barely knew.

His family of two, gone. And then there were three.

* * *

Emma led her army of third graders through the hallway to the gymnasium. She had recess duty, and with the winter storm, their recess would be held inside the gym. Usually, she dreaded snowy days where the kids were crammed inside all day, but after her kiss with Sean, the entire world seems brighter than before. Nothing not even a gym full of rowdy third graders were going to get her down.

Entering the gym, Emma saw she was the first third grade class to arrive. Luckily, recess duty would give her a chance to catch up with Anna.

"Okay class, listen up..." Her third graders were eyeing all the gym equipment, anxious for recess to begin. "Remember, the other third grade class will be joining us, and you'll have to get along and share the equipment. If there is fighting, all the equipment will be put away and the rest of your recess will be a walk and talk. Do you want that to happen?"

"No!" Her entire class groaned.

"Great. Have at it." She motioned for her class to run off for the equipment.

Immediately, the gym erupted into a noisy circus. Anna entered a few moments later with her class, and her kids joined in, raising the volume level another decibel. Emma pointed to the bleachers, and Anna soon joined her on the bottom row, so they could talk, but continue to watch their students.

"How's the morning being going?" Emma took a sip of her drink while tracking her students' interactions.

Anna pulled out a bag of pretzels from her coat pocket to munch on. "Not too bad, considering the kids are trapped inside all day. This recess should help."

Emma crossed her legs. "Agreed."

Anna popped a pretzel into her mouth while Emma sipped her drink. After a few seconds, she said, "I've been dying to know how your date went."

Emma smiled, remembering their heart stopping kiss in

the parking lot. The kiss which helped her forget the mess of the evening.

Glancing sideways at her, Anna laughed. "Was it that good?"

"Yes." Then her eyes picked up a potential fight over the jump ropes. "Sarah and Jude, you better find a way to resolve your fight, or they are gone!" She shouted at them." Both girls froze like they had been caught red-handed.

"Okay, we'll share," said Sarah and Jude in unison.

Once the girls had resolved their fight and appeared to be getting along, Emma continued. "The date was a bit of a fiasco, but it ended well."

"You don't say." Anna's voice rose an octave. "Now I need to know the whole story."

Emma quickly gave the details of the date as the volume in the gym rose. She had to stop every few moments to break up fights over equipment. Finally, she arrived at the good part, where she and Sean kissed. Emma sighed wistfully as her heart fluttered.

Anna's eyes widened. "You what?"

They were interrupted by a student. "Jacob isn't sharing the basketball."

"Tell him he has to share, or it's gone." Anna stated. The child ran off happy to announce to Jacob the letter of the law. She turned back to Emma. "You kissed?"

A smile grew across her face. "Yep. I don't know... Sean's different. For one, he's helping me forget all about Jake..."

Anna piped up. "Exactly. Jake who?" She waved a hand dramatically.

Her being was lighter and freer as Jake slinked further from the front of her mind. Sean was more than a distraction. He might even be... Okay, she was getting way ahead of herself. Crossing her arms, she cleared her throat.

"Also, I really enjoy talking to him. I mean, I can talk to

him about anything, and he *listens*. Jake was horrible at listening. He always was interrupting me. Things are better with Sean in ways I didn't even know were possible."

"I'm so happy for you." Anna grinned, nudging her playfully with her shoulder. "I guess some people have all the luck."

Emma forced a laugh. "I wouldn't say that. I was dumped the night before my wedding. Remember?" She raised an eyebrow. "I think that trumps most people in the romance gone wrong department."

"Touché." Anna picked up a loose ball that stopped right in front of them. She tossed it back in the direction of the group playing four square. "Think about it. You were dumped..." She made a big sweeping motion with her hand. "Then the man of your dreams comes waltzing in to save the day. The two of you go out. There's a spark. The odds of that alone are remarkable. If that's not enough, you share a knee bending kiss. Come on. It's something out of a romance novel."

"Not exactly." She rolled her eyes, cautiously reminding herself to guard her heart. "It was only a kiss. Give it a hot minute. Soon enough, I'll find out his glaringly obvious flaws. Like he eats in bed or saves all his toenail clipping or something equally gross."

"Ewe." Anna made a gag me gesture. "Could you imagine?"

"Yes. Yes, I could. I once dated a guy who ate butter like it was ice cream."

Anna burst out laughing. She doubled over, gripping her chest.

Emma snorted. "I'm glad you find my life so amusing. I've had to live it." She waved it off, changing the subject. "Anyway... we're going maple tapping this weekend. I'll make sure to note everything that pops out at me."

Anna shook her head. "Nah... he sounds perfect." She said, stone faced. They erupted in shared laughter.

The bell rung, ending the chaotic indoor recess. Both stood, collecting their respective classes.

Chapter Nine

Sean couldn't believe the man in front of him was his dad. Thomas was a married man? None of this made any sense. His mind rapidly counted the days since Thomas had last left. It hadn't been all that long. A few months max. People didn't meet someone, fall in love, and get *married* in that span of time. They just didn't.

"You're married?!" Sean hissed.

Calm down, calm down. Calm. Down.

Clinching his jaw, Sean tightened his fists into balls at the side of his body, squeezing with all his might. He willed for his anxious energy to be captured in them and his blood pressure to keep from exploding.

Thomas pulled Lisa protectively closer to him, wrapping his arm around her. She inched next to him, placing her arm around his waist. He gave her a reassuring smile.

"Yes. I'm married." Each word was slow and calculated, indicating Sean was on shaky ground. Thomas pushed up his chin. "I would've told you sooner, but I wanted to tell you in person."

Sean shook his head, running his fingers through his hair. "When? And... how did this happen?"

Lisa flinched.

Thomas raised an eyebrow. "Sean..." The tone sent a chill down his spine.

Sean blinked. "Sorry... I'm having a hard time processing this whole situation." He stepped forward, holding out his hand. "I'm Sean." He forced himself to be cordial.

When did his dad have time to find someone? Let alone marry them? Mind blown. His vision became double. *Focus. Focus.*

Lisa took his hand, shaking it. "I'm Lisa." She smiled brightly back at him. "Your dad has told me so much about you. He's very proud of you."

The words fell flat. Sean's temples were throbbing. He found it hard to concentrate on what Lisa was saying. He blinked. "Is that right?" He scratched his head. "Tell me again, how did you two meet?"

Thomas grinned with a googly eye look.

"Well... it's a funny story." Thomas laughed.

Lisa snorted, putting her hand over her heart. The other gripped Thomas's forearm. "Oh, dear... Yes, you tell him, honey."

Honey? They already had pet names for each other. Perfect.

Thomas caught Sean's eye and stopped laughing with Lisa. "I had gone to a laundry mat outside of Zion National Park." He exchanged a longing glance with Lisa.

"And?" added Sean, in the hopes of moving this entire conversation along.

Lisa added, "long story short... he ended up getting my laundry instead of his own."

Thomas continued where Lisa left off. "After we sorted that all out, I took one look at Lisa and asked her out. It's not every day you meet a beautiful woman, when you spend most of your days driving around in an RV." He pulled Lisa even closer, kissing her on the cheek.

Lisa's cheeks reddened, but she gazed up at Thomas lovingly.

Sean threw his hands up. "That's it? That's the story?"

Thomas beamed. "That's it."

Sean gnawed on his bottom lip, nearly tasting blood. He paused. "Certainly... well... that's a story alright." He spoke slowly emphasizing each word. "I still don't understand what's so hilarious about it."

Lisa laughed, waving it off. "You had to be there."

"Apparently," mumbled Sean.

Thomas slapped Sean on the back with his free hand. "I'll tell you all about it tomorrow at lunch."

"Oh, goody." Sean's lips formed a tight smile. "I can't wait to hear it again." He muttered.

Thomas ignored his sarcasm. "We're tired and have had a long day of driving. We need to call it a night."

"That might be a good idea," stated Sean.

"We'll take you to lunch." Thomas laughed. "Because we can't do breakfast, being newlyweds and all."

Sean closed his eyes for a moment, pinching the bridge of his nose. "Please let this be the end of this conversation," he grumbled.

"Absolutely." Thomas grabbed onto Lisa's hand. Their fingers interlocked. "We'll see you tomorrow."

Lisa headed toward the door and waved. "It was nice meeting you."

Sean managed a nod. "Until tomorrow."

The two of them slipped out into the back parking lot. Their RV hugging the wall of the clinic.

A part of him wanted his dad to be happy. The other part of him selfishly wanted him all to himself. Things were changing, and he didn't like it. Not one bit. He went back to his office, slumping into his desk chair. His mind desperately tried to process the news, but he couldn't settle his thoughts. Whipping out his phone, his fingers slid across the screen without a thought.

Sean: You'll never guess what just happened.

Feeling jittery, Sean paced his office. Waiting for a reply, he replayed the whole interaction with his dad and Lisa. He heard the phone ding. Quickly, he grabbed it off the top of his desk.

Emma: I have no idea. Any hints? Emma followed it with a raised eyebrow emoji.

Sean inhaled, trying his best to calm down.

Sean: Let's just say my dad just dropped some big news on me.

Emma: What is it?

He typed the words which he didn't even believe into his phone.

Sean: My dad showed up today to visit in his RV, and he brought a woman with him.

Emma: Okay...

Sean: The woman is apparently his wife. He eloped.

Sean stretched his neck both ways, waiting for Emma's response. A few seconds later, his phone rang.

"Emma. I'm spiraling." Sean blurted out before she even said hello.

He gathered his things and turned off the lights to his office. He strode through his clinic to the exit.

"Your dad eloped?" asked Emma. He could only imagine the wide-eyed expression she surely was wearing.

He rolled his eyes again at the absurdity of it all. His dad was a grown man, not an eighteen-year-old running off against his parents' wishes.

"No lie. The man is married." His voice lingering over each word. "His new wife is *Lisa*."

"Are you okay?" Her voice was laced with concern. "You seem rather out of sorts."

"No! I'm not okay!" Sean aggressively flipped off the last light in the lobby, then locked the clinic door.

"Alright... back up." Emma cleared her throat. "Calm down... let's talk this whole thing through."

Without thinking, Sean asked, "Why did my dad have to go off and ruin everything by getting married? He knows marriage is not good for anyone. It never works out." He lingered at the bottom of his stairs which led to his apartment. His heartrate picked up to a staccato beat even though he stood still. His mind whirling, he found it hard to remain rational.

Emma didn't respond to his outburst. Silence lingered, palpable, and it made him flinch. Pulling the phone away from his ear, he double checked to make sure the connection. He placed it back to his ear. "Emma, are you still there?" Sean took the stairs two at a time, unlocking his apartment door. He went inside.

"I'm still here." Her voice softer than before.

"What's wrong?" asked Sean. He tossed his stuff onto the kitchen table, then landed on the sofa.

"I...I..." Emma stammered. A tale-tale sign he had messed up, royally. She finally continued. "I'm mulling over your comment on how marriage is not good for anyone... Do you honestly believe that?"

Marriage wasn't worth the risk. So yes, Sean would never walk a woman down the aisle. Ever. No woman was ever going to change his mind. Not even Emma. "It's true. I don't believe in marriage." He stated blatantly. No use in beating around the bush.

With all the problems that came from marriage, he had yet to have someone convince him it wasn't a waste of time and energy. Look at his parents. The two had been miserable together, and then when things were difficult, his mom packed up and left. He was the one who had suffered the most from his parents' choice to marry. In no way, shape, or form, would he ever repeat it.

"You don't believe in marriage?" Emma's voice rose an octave.

He picked up a pillow from the sofa, placing it on his lap to rest his elbow. "I don't."

Marriage was an antiqued institution. No one entered it without knowing how it was most likely going to fail. More than half of marriages ended in divorce. Sean didn't like the odds, nor did he plan on rolling the dice.

"I just... I can't believe this... you seem... like..." Emma's voice faded.

Emma was different from any other woman he had dated, but it didn't change how he felt. Witnessing his dad act like he had been hit by cupid's arrow today had only deepened his resolve. He was digging in his heals. Anyone he dated needed to know he would never marry them.

"I'm sorry, Emma. It's how I feel. I won't get married. It's not that big of a deal, many people never marry." Sean stated.

He held his breath, hoping it didn't change what he had found with Emma. He enjoyed being around her, talking to her. Then there was the kissed they shared. It made his head spin whenever he thought about it.

"I can't believe that's how you feel... but if that's the case..." Emma paused, clearing her throat. "Let's go ahead and cancel our date for this weekend. It would be a waste of time for the both of us."

His heart dropped. He sat straight up, waving his hand. "No. No, don't do that. We're just beginning to get to know each other." Sean ran his free hand through his hair. "There's no need to get all dramatic about this. We enjoy each other's company can't we just leave it at that?"

"No." The word sliced through him. When Emma continued, her voice had an icy edge. "That won't work for me. I want to get married. I can't waste my time dating someone who doesn't want the same things as me."

The vein in his temple throbbed, and he pinched the bridge of his nose. "Please don't. I just had the shock of my life." Even though he had only known Emma for a little while, he didn't want to lose her. He liked her, connected with her deeper than anyone else he had met in the past. "Let's not make any more decisions about this tonight."

"Have you suddenly changed your mind about marriage in the last two minutes?"

"I haven't." He closed his eyes, dreading the words she would speak next.

"That's what I thought. Sean... it was a pleasure meeting you. Best of luck with your dad and his new wife."

The phone went dead. Sean pulled the phone away from his ear. The call ended and returned to his screensaver. Tossing his phone on top of his sofa, he leaned forward running his hand down his face. In the past, when he revealed this to someone he was dating, usually the woman brushed it off as no big deal. Part of him knew they saw his non-marrying ways as a challenge, thinking they would be the woman to make him change his mind. It had yet to happen.

Emma's reaction had caught him completely off guard. Instead of reacting like all the other women in his past, she had canceled their date, ended whatever was beginning between the two of them. His middle soured. Truth be, he hadn't known Emma all that long, so why did he feel this disappointed?

* * *

The next morning, he walked through his clinic door, late and grumpy. He hadn't slept at all, only tossed and turned. His conversation with Emma had played on repeat in his mind. The fact that his dad had eloped with Lisa seemed to be the least of his worries.

"Good morning." He forced a tight smile as he greeted Julie.

Glancing up from her desk, she greeted him. With a mail opener in one hand, and a huge envelope in the other, she continued. "Did your dad make it in okay?"

Sean mulled over how to respond. Did he spoil the surprise? Nah. This was something he would've paid good money to see. "Sure did." He smiled brightly, faking a pleasant mood. "You'll get to see him later today, because he's stopping by to take me to lunch."

"Great. Can't wait." Julie cheerfully replied.

"You're in for a real surprise." Sean mumbled under his breath.

"What was that?" she asked, confused.

Sean waved his hand, forcing another smile. "Nothing. When's my first appointment?"

Julie reached over, moving the cursor on her computer screen. Her eyes scanned the screen. "Three minutes. Mr. Bridges' bunny."

"Will do. I'll go drop my stuff in my office, and I'll be right back." Sean made his way down the hallway to his office, unpacking what he brought with him for the day.

Before he had time to think, Julie popped her head into the doorway of his office and handed him a file. "He's here."

"Great." He clapped his hands together, trying to focus his mind on his job and patients.

The rest of the morning sped by, and next thing he knew, it was lunch. Lingering in the lobby, he waited for his dad to arrive.

Spotting Thomas and Lisa through the lobby window, he peered over his shoulder toward Julie. "I see my dad coming." He announced to the empty waiting room.

Shifting in her seat, Julie asked, "He is?"

Then she stood, walking toward the window. She peered outside. "Who is that?! Why is your dad holding hands with someone?" Julie gripped onto his forearm, searching his face for more information. "You knew about this, and you didn't tell me!" She released her grip, shaking her head. "I can't believe you."

Sean smirked. "I thought it would be more fun for you to find out this way."

Julie shook a finger at him. "I want to ring your neck that you withheld this from me."

"And that isn't even all of it," he mumbled.

Julie's jaw dropped, but Thomas and Lisa entered the clinic before the two could discuss it any further.

"Thomas!" exclaimed Julie. Clapping her hands together excitedly, she then held her arms out for a hug. "It's so good to see you."

Lisa took a slight step out of the way, quietly watching their embrace.

Thomas put his hand at the small of Lisa's back. "Julie, I wanted to introduce you to my wife, Lisa." Thomas winked at Lisa.

A shocked expression crossed Julie's face, quickly replaced by a tight smile. She looked between the pair and Sean. At least he wasn't the only one shocked and throw off by his dad's news.

"Your wife?" Julie clasped her hands tightly together. "Okay. How 'bout that?" The words slightly forced.

"Yes. My wife," said Thomas, beaming with pride.

Biting down on her lip, Julie nodded slowly. She waved her hands and smiled warmly at the couple. "I... I think that's wonderful." She held out her hand to Lisa. "I'm Julie. I was Thomas' secretary for years, and now I work for his son."

Lisa took the outstretched hand, smiling. "Nice to meet you. Thomas has told me all about you and the clinic." She shuffled her feet. Thomas wrapped his arm around her shoulders.

Julie teased, "I hope only good things."

Lisa grinned. "Of course."

Sean glanced at his watch, interrupting. "Dad, I think we better get going. I only have an hour before my next client."

"Of course. Let's go." Thomas with Julie in tow moved toward the door. "It was great seeing you again," he added.

Julie smiled. "Yes... and congrats. Have a nice lunch." She returned to her desk.

Thomas opened the door, holding it open. "After you two..."

The three of them left, walking a few blocks to their favorite sandwich shop. A place Sean and Thomas had frequented far too many times to count over the years.

After they ordered and received their food, they settled into a booth. Thomas and Lisa saddled up to each other on one side, leaving Sean to stare at them from across the table.

After a few failed attempts by Thomas to start a conversation with him, Sean dug deep, trying his best to not act like a spoiled toddler. "Where are you from, Lisa?" He took a bite of his French dip sandwich. "I mean... before you met my dad, did you travel around the world in an RV, too?"

Lisa took a sip of her soda before responding. "I kind of grew up all over, mainly in the Midwest." She nervously brought her hands onto her lap, rubbing them over the top of her thighs. Her eyes meekly met his, melting Sean's hardened heart. The woman seemed nice enough, maybe with time he would even learn to tolerate the idea of his dad being married.

"Really?" Sean nodded. "You don't say."

"I don't normally even camp." Lisa peered between Sean and Thomas. "I was on a two-week camping trip with my girlfriends when I met your dad outside of Zion."

Thomas placed his hand on top of hers. "Luckily, she and her girlfriends took pity on me as a lonely bachelor. They invited me to go on a hike with them. Lisa and I hit it off right from the start."

Lisa leaned over and patted him on the thigh. "We sure did. Didn't we?" She made eyes at him, and they exchanged smiles.

There was no denying it. They looked happy together. Sean didn't know why it irritated him, grating on his nerves. Surely, his dad deserved to be happy. Didn't he? Yes... but the possible ramifications could be astronomical. Eloping... come on, that was something eighteen-year-olds did, not a man in his sixties.

"That's right, honey." Thomas leaned in and kissed Lisa lightly on the lips. "It was love at first sight."

Lisa sighed wistfully. Then Thomas leaned in and kissed her again. Sean stared back at them in horror. He had never seen his dad kiss anyone, not even his mom. Thomas had changed. Sean was no longer his source of happiness like it was before. He had been pushed aside.

Inhaling, Sean ran his fingers through his hair. "That's certainly a story..." he stated, loudly.

The two stopped kissing, turning their attention back to him. "A real love story." Thomas added enthusiastically.

Sean fiddled with his pack of chips. His mind was a muddled mess. Leaning forward, he rubbed his face, desperately trying to process this entire thing. Without thinking, he blurted out, "I mean, going on a hike together is one thing... eloping well... that's an entirely different animal." He immediately regretted his rashness.

Devastated, Lisa's face became crest fallen. Her lips

forming a perfectly straight line. "Well...I..." She glanced nervously over at Thomas.

Thomas narrowed his eyes at Sean. He had crossed a line, and he knew it. "To others, it might seem like a leap, but I love Lisa." He kissed her on the temple and spoke with an air of confidence. "Marrying her was the best decision I've ever made."

Lisa beaming, she stared back at Thomas and ignored Sean. "Best decision I've ever made." Then she leaned over and kissed him.

The rest of the meal continued with stilted conversation. Sean tried to back pedal, to right the wrong he had so bluntly made. It was fruitless. All knew he didn't approve of them getting married.

His shoulders drooped as they walked back to the clinic. Lisa excused herself to peruse some of the shops on Main Street. Father and son alone for the first time, Sean frantically tried to think of what to say, but he came up empty.

Neither spoke the rest of the way. In front of the clinic, Thomas broke the silence, lingering in front of the door.

"Before you go, there are a few things I need to say."

Gulping, Sean met his dad's gaze. "Okay..."

Thomas crossed his arms. "Now, son, you've made it perfectly clear of how you don't approve of me marrying Lisa..."

Sean lowered his eyes. "It's... just... that." He stumbled over his words.

Thomas continued. "I will not allow you to treat Lisa like that ever again. You might not like what I did, but I won't tolerate you treating her poorly. Do you understand?"

"I'm sorry." He looked over at him. "I misspoke. It won't happen again." Sean plunged his hands into his pocket.

Warmly, Thomas smiled. "Great." He held his arms open

for an embrace. The two hugged. "It was great seeing you." He patted him on the back.

"Thanks for coming to visit." Sean reached for the door, wanting this whole interaction to be over. For him to have time to warm up to the whole idea of his dad being a married man, alone. "I wish you the best with Lisa. I really do." He wished he meant it.

"Thanks, son." Thomas grinned. "She makes me so happy. I can't remember ever feeling like this."

"I'm glad." Sean crossed the threshold of the clinic. "See you soon, dad."

"Bye." Thomas waved, pivoting in the direction of where Lisa was shopping.

Brushing off the awkward lunch, Sean went to finish the rest of his workday. As much as he hoped his dad had finally found happiness, he knew his dad would be lucky if the marriage lasted a year. Because after all, second marriages had an even worse track record than firsts.

Chapter Ten

The bright light from the sunrise peeked through the curtains of Emma's bedroom. Groaning, she flipped to her other side, not wanting to get up. She lost sleep while her conversation with Sean played on repeat in her mind. The man infuriated her. Previously, he had expressed some reservations about marriage, but she hadn't known he never wanted to get married, ever. She wondered if all his hang-ups came from his mom abandoning him. It likely played a huge role, but why was he letting it determine his whole future?

Covering her eyes with the crook of her elbow, she blocked out the sun, hoping for a few more minutes of sleep. Sean. Sean. Sean. The man had been a welcome distraction. The one who managed to take her heart off of Jake, making her believe she might find someone new someday. Smiling, she remembered their kiss in the parking lot. She sighed. It had just been a kiss, one that left her knees weak and breathless, but not one to fuss over. No more Sean. No more Jake. The reality of her singledom came crashing down on her once more. Snuggling under her covers, she chose to hide from reality a little longer.

After a lazy Sunday morning, she knew eventually she

would need to get out of bed. Sunday meant Sunday dinner with her parents. If she didn't show, they would meddle and worry. Reluctantly, she pulled back the covers of her bed. Removing the warm comforter from her body, the winter air pierced her skin, awakening her senses. She shivered as she walked to her bathroom to shower. For a long time, she stood under the scolding water to smooth out the stiff feeling in her neck and shoulders.

After toweling off, she stood in front of the steamy bathroom mirror. Reaching out, she wiped a portion of the mirror with her hand. Her skin was still pink from the piping hot water and her once vibrant eyes had taken on a lackluster tone. Leaning forward, she gripped the edge of the vanity with her hands to give herself the proper pep talk. "Pull it together or they'll never stop worrying about you." She spoke to her image in the mirror. "They have to believe you're okay."

Whether she liked it or not, her parents were concerned about her well-being. Deep down she appreciated their support, but she wondered when they were would think she was healed. Though she was far from okay, she simply needed her parents to see her happy again.

Knuckles turning white, she gripped the vanity with full force. "You can do this." The words echoed in the small space, vibrating all around her. Seeping into her veins, she almost believed them. Believed she was over Jake. Believed there was still hope in the world. Believed someday she would find a better, more perfect fit. Be over the quick and random encounter with Sean.

Despite her dreary state, she left the bathroom to dress in her newest outfit, surprising herself when she applied makeup and did her hair. By the time she arrived at her parents' house, she was almost feeling normal.

Her dad, Noah, opened the front door before she even

had time to ring the doorbell. "How's my favorite daughter?" asked Noah. He pulled her in for a hug.

"Great," replied Emma, as she plastered a weak smile across her face. "Your only daughter, I might add."

Noah laughed, releasing his embrace. He gave her a once over. Emma smiled her biggest and brightest.

Noah spoke slowly. "You do look better today." A surprise look crossed his face, one Emma failed to read. "Maybe you are starting to get over what's-his-bucket?"

She groaned, speaking through gritted teeth, her jaw locked. "Jake. You know his name."

Noah motioned for her to follow him inside, and she trailed along behind him. He spoke over his shoulder, as they made their way down the hallway toward the kitchen.

"That's right. Jake." His shoulders tensed, his eyes narrowing. "I'm doing my best to forget that good for nothing. I'm almost there."

Emma nodded in agreement. "I want to forget him, too." She bit down on her bottom lip, tears forming in the corner of her eyes. Swallowing, she blinked rapidly, willing herself to remain steady. "Dad, I'm trying."

Her words stopped her dad straight in his tracks. Pivoting, he met her eyes square on. "I know you are, honey. You'll get over him. I promise." He reached out, patting her arm. "Someday, it won't feel this hard."

She forced a smile. "Thanks, dad. I really hope so."

The two continued to the kitchen, where Melanie was placing the last of the food on the dining table. Lemon roasted chicken with potatoes and carrots. A staple in their household for Sunday dinner. The smell was intoxicating, and Emma remembered how she had barely eaten since her conversation with Sean the night before. Her appetite came back with a vengeance, mouthwatering.

Emma sat down at dining table. "Mom, the food smells delicious."

"Thanks. I made your favorite. Comfort food," said Melanie, as she placed her napkin in her lap.

"I sure could use some comfort," added Emma.

Noah joined, taking his place next to Melanie. "I heard you are on to bigger and better. Some new guy?" he raised an eyebrow.

Emma inhaled, closing her eyes for a moment. "That whole thing ended." She waved it off. "Nothing new to report."

Melanie reached for the glass pitcher, filling her cup. "What's this about?" Her voice rose an octave. "Things have fizzled with Sean?"

"It's not a big deal." Emma shrugged but fiddled with her hands under the table. "Things didn't work out... last night over the phone, Sean revealed he never planned on getting married. It's a deal breaker for me, so I ended things. Not that we were really a thing, we barely knew one another."

"He never wants to get married?" Melanie reached for Noah's hand while her other hand sprung to her heart.

Nonchalantly, Emma served herself some of the carrots. "Nope. Do you mind passing the potatoes?"

With a void look, Melanie mindlessly complied. Emma took the plate from her, serving herself. Next, she loaded her plate with some of the chicken.

Melanie frozen, eyed her daughter. "Ever?"

Emma finished serving herself. "Ever." Digging into her plate, she took a bite of the meat. It melted in her mouth, juicy and tender. The familiar taste gratified her rumbling stomach. "It's not a big deal. No harm, no foul. He was a nice distraction. Nothing more."

Melanie remained still, unmoving. She opened her mouth to speak but stopped, shaking her head.

Trying to change the subject, Emma pointed to her mouth. "Mom, this is excellent. Thanks for making my favorite."

Noah finished serving his food and began to eat. "Yes, honey. You out did yourself this time. It tastes great."

Melanie leaned back in her chair, folding her arms. Her plate remained empty. "I can't get over that. Sean's such a nice guy being a vet an all..." She made a tsk sound with her tongue. "I thought he was the poster child for a family man."

"I know." Emma agreed. Shoving the carrots closer to Melanie, she gave her a pointed look. "Eat. This is good. You worked hard. No use in letting your food get cold." Anything to drop the subject of Sean.

"Come on, honey. Eat. Don't worry. Emma will find a nice guy soon enough." Noah reached out, giving Melanie's hand a squeeze. "Someday, when the time is right." He gave Emma an encouraging smile.

She gave a curt nod in return and continued to eat.

Melanie began to load up her plate with the food. "I really liked him." She shook her head again. "Such a shame."

"Okay, mom. Let's drop it." Emma narrowed her eyes. "You're acting like you wanted to date him."

Noah let out a belly laugh, his hand whipping to his chest.

Flustered, Melanie took a bite of her carrots. "Don't be absurd. I'm doing no such thing."

Emma laughed along with her dad.

Melanie threw up her hands. "Okay. I'll drop the whole Sean thing."

Emma cleared her throat, taking a sip of her water. "I haven't heard about your trip. Tell me all about it."

Her parents had recently gone to Maine for a few days. Both of her parents had retired last year, which meant most of their time was spent traveling around the world together. After all these years, they still enjoyed one another's company and being together. Retirement only brought her parents closer. Their love story encouraged her to not give up on her quest to find love.

Melanie's face lit up. "You haven't heard about our trip." She smiled lovingly at Noah. "It was wonderful."

"Truly. Maine is beautiful. I can't believe with us living on the east coast all our lives, we haven't gone up there more," added Noah.

Emma continued to prod them with questions about their trip. Anything to convince them she was slowly getting over Jake, healing and moving forward.

After the meal, Noah walked Emma out to her car. Lingering, he shoved his hands into his pockets. "I hope you are doing okay, kiddo." His brow burrowed. "I worry about you."

"I know, dad," said Emma. The sun was long gone. The darkness of winter made her shiver. She tugged her jacket together, zipping it up. "It's okay. But I'm fine. Really, I am." The words sounded overly forced, even to her.

He reached out, bringing her into an embrace. "You're not." Noah whispered into her ear. "But... you will be. I promise. You are stronger than you believe."

The words brought tears to her eyes. Hugging him until she regained her composure. "Thanks, dad." She whispered back. "I sure hope so."

He stepped back. "I love you. It'll get better. Just give it time. A year from now, all of this will be in your rearview mirror."

"I love you, dad." Emma wiped the last of the stray tears off her cheeks. She moved toward her car. "I'll see you next week."

Opening her car door for her, Noah waited for her settle in her seat. "I'll see you then."

Noah stood in the driveway, watching her pull her away.

She considered her dad's words, knowing she wasn't okay, but she would be someday.

The tears started again. In full force, streaming down her cheeks and blurring her vision. Shoulders shaking, she pulled the car to the side of the road. Leaning on the steering wheel, she sobbed.

A good amount of time passed. Eventually, she managed to pull herself together. Digging around in her glove box, she found some left-over fast-food napkins and blew her nose. With nothing left to do, she merged back onto the road and drove home, hoping that with enough time Jake... and Sean would be in her rearview mirror.

Chapter Eleven

"Did your dad and his new wife..." Julie nudged him playfully with her elbow. "Make it off okay yesterday?"

Julie and Sean stood in line at the pharmacy to fill prescriptions he needed for some of his appointments out of town in the afternoon. Julie was going to drop off the rest of the local ones when he was out on his house calls. The door-to-door service helped bring in new customers and expand the business. Since taking over from his dad, Sean had made a lot of changes, and luckily Julie had been supportive.

"They sure did." Sean tried to keep his voice level. "Him and Lisa are headed to Canada."

Julie's eyes lit up like fireworks on the fourth of July. "I still can't believe your dad's married." Her voice lingered on the last word. "I wouldn't have guessed that for a million dollars."

He rolled his eyes. "You're telling me." Sean couldn't help but grumble.

She tilted her head to the side. "I'm really happy for him," Julie stated, as if she dared him to argue.

Sean exhaled, his shoulders drooping. "I wish I could be, but I'm in shock."

"I... never mind." Julie glanced away.

"Spill it. What is it?" Sean shifted his weight. The line moved, and both shuffled forward.

"I remember how awful it was after your mom up and left." Julie smiled at someone she knew who passed by them in the aisle. She waited until they were out of earshot to continue. "I'm glad he has someone again in his life."

"I know he deserves to be happy." Sean wrung his hands together, capturing his anxiety. "But you forget my mom left me, too."

And he had the emotional scars to prove it. All his issues always traveled back to the woman who didn't love him. Part of him questioned any woman ever loving him enough to stay, especially when it became messy and difficult. It was easy to love someone when things were easy and perfect, but what about all the other times? When life throws you curve balls, would they high tail it? *Emma would stay. Emma could be the one who was different.* He pushed Emma far from his mind.

Julie continued. "Very true. I don't deny the damage she reaped, but your dad shielded you from the worst of it." She peered out the window overlooking Main Street. "He did his best to create a stable home for you. When you were still young and at home, he didn't date half the town trying to find another woman. He waited because he knew how fragile you were..." She brought her gaze back to him. "Now you're a grown man. It's time to be an adult. Let your dad be happy."

"Yikes." He recoiled at his apparent selfishness. "You certainly aren't beating around the bush."

The line moved again. They only had one person in front of them. "Your dad has had a hard life. I watched all of it unfold. This is his chance at happiness." She raised an eyebrow. "I mean, have you ever seen him look that happy?"

His dad was a man of few words. A calm and steady force in his life. This was the first time he had seen his dad this full of life. It had to be Lisa, but who knew how long this whole marriage would last? A year? What would happen to his dad if it didn't work out?

"He did look happy... I can't deny it," said Sean slowly.

"I'm glad your dad found someone. He deserves it." Julie lightly touched him on his arm. "Your dad loves you so much. If you don't accept Lisa, it will kill him."

The words sliced through Sean. His dad had been the one to stay, the one who sacrificed for him to have all he did. Of course, he made some mistakes, but he hadn't abandoned him. Not like his mom.

Sean cleared his throat, embarrassed by his behavior. "I do want him to find joy again, but the whole thing has rattled me."

Julie chuckled, lightening the mood between them. "You could've blown me away."

It was their turn. Both step in front of the pharmacy counter. The pharmacist knew him well and began gathering the large number of prescriptions. They stepped to the side to wait. After waiting for a few minutes, Julie asked, "I almost forgot. How did the maple tapping date go with Emma?"

The mention of Emma made his shoulders stiffen. The woman up and ran the minute he mentioned he didn't want to get married. It was a mystery to him why they couldn't continue to see each other, keeping things nice and casual.

Sean shuffled his feet, fiddling with the paper in his hands. "We didn't end up going out."

Her eyes widened, voice rising an octave. "What happened?"

Sean ran his free hand through his hair, biting down on his bottom lip. "I happened to mention how I never wanted to get married, and she told me us going out again would be a waste of her time."

Julie made a tsk sound, shaking her head. "That would do it." She pointed her finger at him. "You deserved her cancelling on you." She folded her arms and looked away.

"You think I deserved her cancelling on me?" Evidently, all women had some sort of creed they closely followed.

"You heard me." Julie kept her stare on the pharmacy. "She doesn't have time to waste on a boy like you. The woman wants to find a good and decent man. Not a guy who acts like a child." She pushed up her chin.

Sean paused, pondering her words. "You think I'm acting like a *child?*" He dropped his hands at his side dramatically.

"Yes." Julie sighed. Then she peered back at him. "When are you going to get over your hang-ups with women? Your mom left you years ago. Your dad is finally moving on. Don't you think it's time to move on, too? Time to find a nice woman to settle down with, one who *will* stay. Some marriages last. People can stay in love." Her voice lowered. "I wish I could help you see how much you're holding yourself back from happiness."

The words bounced off him, failing to land. Why did she care who he dated? He loved and respected Julie like a mother, but she didn't know what it was like to be him. He believed he was unlovable. Scared beyond measure, he worried that whomever he chose to love might not love him back or one day they might wake up and walk away. "Well... You certainly have given me some things to think about."

Julie's lips formed a tight line, and she curtly nodded, but remained quiet.

If only he could forget all about Emma. Forget about the way her lips glided over his. How the world stood still for a moment and made him forget about all those he had kissed before. If he was kissing anyone, he wanted it to be Emma. Only her.

The pharmacist announced their orders, breaking their silence, and they went their separate ways.

* * *

Monday morning, after an incredibly long and depressing weekend, Emma pulled into her school parking lot. Relieved for something to occupy her thoughts, she knew she could trust teaching to take her mind off what could never be.

Anna pulled into the space next to her and waved through the window. They both got out at the same time.

Smiling, Emma called out to Anna from her car door. "Good morning, Anna."

She reached back into her car, grabbing an arm full of books, then shut her car door. Bundled up with thick wool gloves and scarf, the winter air nipped at her skin. To stay warm, she shuffled her feet while she waited for Anna to gather the rest of her things.

Anna strode toward Emma. "How was your weekend?" she asked as she adjusted her purse strap on her shoulder.

"Fine. Quiet." Emma kept her gaze steady on the ground in front of her, taking slow and deliberate steps on the slick pavement. The last thing she needed was a broken bone.

"Quiet?" Anna matched her speed, taking small ginger steps. "I thought you were going maple tapping with Sean."

Emma exhaled, shaking her head. "We didn't end up going out." She braced herself for the questions which would follow.

"What! You didn't go?" Anna asked a little too loudly. She lowered her tone to a more normal level. "Why not? What happened?"

At the front of the school, Anna opened the door, and Emma followed her inside. The heat was cranked up. Emma tugged at her scarf to loosen it from her neck while trying to balance the books in her arms. Next, she pulled off her gloves with her teeth.

"I found out he never wants to get married."

Anna gasped, then made a tsk sound with her tongue. "Really? Well, that's just sad." She cocked her head to the side. "Who doesn't want to get married?"

"Men, that's who," grumbled Emma.

She shoved her gloves into her coat pocket, wiggling out her keys. They stopped in front of her classroom. She unlocked it, lingering in front of the threshold.

"Not all men," replied Anna, cheerfully.

The enthusiasm in her voice made Emma raise an eyebrow. "What?" She searched her face for understanding.

Anna smiled meekly. "Not all men are like Jake or Sean." She pushed up her chin. "Some do want to get married."

"Okay... What's going on here?" Emma folded her arms. "Usually, you're complaining about how Ben is never going to ask you to marry him."

Grinning, Anna wiggled her ring finger in front of Emma so she could see the sparkly ring. It was big and dazzling. The thing practically blinded her.

Emma gasped. "You're engaged!" She practically screamed. Grabbing Anna's hand, she stared down at the brilliant round stone and examined it closer. "Congratulations. It's gorgeous. You could see that baby from outer space."

Anna laughed. "Thanks." Beaming, she held her hand out in front of herself, admiring her engagement ring. "Ben saved for a long time to get me the ring I wanted. That's why it took him so long to propose."

Emma clapped her hands together. "Congrats." She held her arms out for an embrace. Hugging, she continued. "I'm so happy for you."

"Thanks. I didn't mean for you to find out this way, but I

wanted to tell you in person." A look of concern crossed her face. "I... I hope this..."

Emma waved her hand, interrupting Anna. "No. Stop. I'm nothing but happy for you. No need to tiptoe around me."

Anna's shoulders cowered. "I know things are still painful for you."

Reaching out, Emma grabbed Anna's arm. "I'm fine. This is a happy day!"

A smile crept across Anna's face. "There are still some good ones out there. Don't give up hope." She glanced down at her finger with its sparkling diamond the size of Texas, sighing contently. "I'm sure you'll find your prince charming someday."

"Maybe." Emma forced a smile, which she hoped looked genuine.

Anna glanced at her watch. "I've got to run, because I need to pick up some things from the office before the bell rings, but we're having an engagement party this weekend, and I want you to come."

Emma nodded. "Absolutely. I'll be there."

So... her friend was getting married. She wished it didn't make her stomach clench and heart sink. Wished more than anything that someday the sadness in her life would dissipate. She still held onto hope that someday she might get her happily ever after, too. It was the only thing moving her forward.

Entering her classroom, Emma slinked into her desk chair. Defeated, she threw her face in her hands. Her friend deserved every bit of happiness, and she was thrilled Anna had finally received a ring after dating Ben for so long.

It wasn't that at all.

It was that she was miserable.

Like so miserable, she hated being around happy people.

Her very presence oozed discontent. She knew she brought a dark cloud of gloom wherever she traveled. How long would she feel like this?

With a swivel of her chair, she turned to face the windows overlooking the playground. Some children had already arrived for school and were playing on the gym equipment and running around on the snow-covered grass. The gleeful sounds of their laughter brought a tiny smile to her face. The corners of her mouth lifting, despite her weary spirit. Breathing in, she bathed in the joy of their carefree play. The innocence of childhood, free from the complications of adulthood.

Emma considered things not working out with Jake or Sean, and she tried convincing herself things ending before she was heavily invested was a blessing.

The bell rung. Rising from her chair, she adjusted her dress. Exhaling, the tightness in her chest loosened. Someday, she would find the right person, because even after all this, she was somebody who still believed in love.

Chapter Twelve

Sean peered back at his cell phone and reread the text from his old college roommate, Ben. Double checking the address to the restaurant, he located the sign above the building. The two matched, confirming he was in the correct location. He slid his cell phone back into his pants pocket, and adjusted his tie and sports coat.

At the beginning of the week, Ben had called to tell him the happy news of his engagement. They had been undergrads together. After graduation, Ben went off to medical school while he ventured onto vet school. Over the years, they had stayed in touch. Meeting up occasionally as time allowed because they both had stayed on the East Coast.

Quickly, over the phone, the two caught up with one another, then he finally got around to the reason Ben was calling in the first place. He wanted to invite him to his engagement party. Yet another one of his friends was taking the dreaded plunged. Though he wasn't a ringing endorsement for the antiquated institution, he was happy to go and celebrate with his friend.

Entering the restaurant, he checked in with the host to

find the private room where the engagement party was being held. All the guests in the crowded room were mingling around cocktail tables and eating hors d'oeuvres from the servers circling the room with silver trays. Sean squinted his eyes as he tried to adjust to the low lighting, searching for Ben. After a few moments, he spotted him in a corner, holding hands with his new fiancée, Anna. They were visiting with some of the other guests. Wandering over to where they stood, Sean waited for them to finish up their conversation before giving his well wishes to the happy couple.

Ben smiled brightly as Sean approached. "Thanks for coming!"

"Congratulations." Sean and Ben embraced. "I'm so happy for you both." Sean looked at Anna, who Ben quickly introduced while beaming with pride as he wrapped his arm around her shoulders.

Ben and Anna locked eyes with one another and for a moment, just two people in their own little love bubble. Sean believed they forgot he was even there, until Ben further explained to Anna how he knew Sean.

"We know each other from way back in our undergrad days," Sean added.

She raised an eyebrow, smirking at Ben. "Is that right?" She nudged him playfully with her elbow. "I guess you could give me some good dirt on him. Right?"

Sean chuckled. "You have no idea." A server came by and offered them food.

"Be kind, Sean." Ben gave him a pointed look then took a bite. "Remember, I have dirt on you, too."

Sean nodded his head in agreement. "That you do, my friend." He grabbed a drink from another tray and cleared his throat. "Really, Anna, I only have good things to say about Ben. He's a great guy. You have nothing to worry about."

Anna squeezed Ben's hand, gazing up at him with loving

eyes. "I know. I found a good one." The two shared a kiss, and Sean remembered kissing Emma. His body ached to hold her near, and then he brushed the thought aside.

Ben slapped him on the back. "It was great seeing you. I've some other people I need to go and say hello to. If you'll excuse us for a minute, we can catch up more later."

Sean waved them off. "Yes. Of course, go."

"It was nice meeting you." Anna added with a smile.

Sean mirrored her smile with a slight nod.

The two walked off hand in hand, quickly fading into the group of friends and family gathered in the room. Awkwardly, he scanned the crowd for any familiar faces. Perhaps some old college friends. After a sweep, he failed to spot a single other person he knew. Feeling out of place, he stepped back out of the way, leaning up against the wall of the packed room.

Another server came by with a plate of meatballs. Sean grabbed one off the plate, shoving it into his mouth. He stared out at the other guests, he decided if he didn't see anyone else he recognized, he would slip out the side door and call it a night.

Shifting his weight on his feet, he took in the party, watching all the happy interactions. Then, he spotted her, entering in a black cocktail dress with her hair curled and bouncy. Emma. His chest tightened. Placing his hand over his heart, Sean forced himself to focus on breathing. His middle pooled, warming. He regretted stuffing his mouth full of meatballs.

To him, Emma was the most beautiful woman in the room. Unable to move, his legs wobbly, he continued to sip his drink as his gaze tracked her from his station against the wall. Every single part of him wanted to talk to her, hold her, kiss her. The longing made his head spin. What was wrong with him? *Move before you miss your chance.* His legs didn't listen, refusing to budge. His heart continued its staccato beat, making his hands clammy.

After Emma scanned the crowded room, she spotted Ben and Anna. Sean watched from the safety of his hidden place as she made her way over to them. Embracing, the three chatted with each other. Blissfully unaware of his presence, Sean wondered what his next move should be. The fact they both knew the happy couple was a remarkable coincidence. Something which someone might conjure up to destiny, more than pure providence, something written in the stars. Shaking his head, he stopped his train of thought. He wasn't a man who believed in any of those romantic notions, or at least he didn't before he met Emma. Seeing her again was making him question everything.

With only one chance to make things right between them, he sipped his drink and racked his brain for a solution. Yearning to speak to her, to repair their newly formed but quickly fractured relationship, he waited and watched until he found the perfect moment to take his chance.

The three of them chatted a little while longer. Soon Anna and Ben were pulled elsewhere leaving her abandoned. Emma shuffled her feet, fluffing her hair. Her dress hugged her body in all the right places, making her hips sway as she moved through the crowd toward the drink table.

Sean threw back the rest of his drink, setting the empty glass on one of the empty cocktail tables. *Game time.* Buttoning his sports jacket, he moved toward her. Emma was still unaware of him being there. *Deep breaths, deep breaths.*

The server held her drink out to her. Emma grabbed it, then turned around right into Sean, almost spilling her drink on him.

Emma gasped, clutching her chest. "Sean?" She nearly bumped into him again. "What are you doing here?" She looked everywhere, nervously avoiding his gaze. Emma tightened her grasp around her drink to keep it from spilling.

"Emma." He smiled, hoping it would break the ice. "What a pleasant surprise to see you here."

Anxiously, she shifted her weight after being bumped into by another guest trying to order a drink. "I don't understand. How do you know Anna?"

He cupped his ear to hear her in the crowded room, leaning closer and catching a whiff of her perfume. The smell nearly did him in. His knees weakening from the intoxicating scent, his mind a muddled mess.

Emma stepped closer, then she was practically pushed up against him by the throng of people.

"Let's get out of here," Sean suggested, reaching for her hand and intertwining their fingers. When they moved through the room toward an empty corner, Sean considered how his skin warmed from her touch, but Emma pulled away, taking a sip from her drink.

She watched the party while he explained how he knew Ben from undergrad, reluctantly following Emma's gaze.

"What a weird coincidence," Emma noted, her voice flat.

His head was spinning. Sean found it hard to concentrate on their conversation. Emma was a beauty on a normal day, but tonight, she was a total knockout. His judgement was questionable. Being this intimately close to her was making him question all his life's decisions.

"How do you know them?" Sean tilted his head toward her, allowing himself another glance.

Without looking at him, she responded. "I work with Anna. She's the other teacher in my grade, and our rooms are right next to each other."

She wasn't going to make this conversation easy. Clearly, she was simply tolerating him because she had yet to recognize someone else. The minute she did, he was positive she would beeline it, leaving him alone.

Sean cringed at his lame attempt to carry on a conversation. "It must be nice to have a friend you work with."

Her icy feelings toward him rocked him all the way to his core. He liked Emma and didn't realize how much until this very night. The woman was beautiful and intriguing. A calming force. Part of him longed to be around her, even if they could only continue being friends. "How long have you known each other?"

"About seven or eight years." She took another sip of her drink, then the worry lines on her forehead softened slightly. "She's made teaching at my school enjoyable. I really am lucky to have a friend at work."

Tracking her eyeline, he pulled his gaze from her to what had caught her eye and made her shoulders drop. She was watching Ben and Anna. The happy couple were exchanging another kiss.

Taking a drink, Sean stated, "I bet this is hard for you."

"What?" Startled by his comment, Emma finally faced him her eyes narrowing. "Why would you say that?" Her tone was accusatory.

He shook his head, seeing her pain and wishing he had kept his observation to himself.

"Sorry, I shouldn't have said that." He scratched his head. "I know you are happy for them, but I also know you're mending a broken heart."

"What would you know about my heart?" Emma folded her arms across her body and pushed up her chin. Her icy glare sent a shiver down his spine.

He gulped. "Not enough... obviously." This conversation was headed down a road he didn't want to travel, and he hoped he could right the course. "I... I just want you to know that you'll get your happily ever after, too."

Emma rolled her eyes. "Well, I do worry." She made a tsk sound with her tongue. "If all the men left are like you, then I'm in trouble."

Sean cringed, wishing for the first time he wasn't a love skeptic. He wished he could be the man she needed. Someone who didn't run away when things became serious.

"I deserved that... but... it's not you, Emma. You're beautiful, gracious, and kind. Any guy would be lucky to have you." His words hung in the air between them, lacing his heart to hers more than he cared to admit.

Sliding his back on the wall, he moved closer to her. Their bodies a mere inch from each other. Not touching, but dangerously close. The impalpable barricade set due to his hang-ups, his inability to let someone know him, all of him. His whole body ached to close the gap and draw her next to him. Though he never wanted to marry, she was the one he wanted. The one, when he pushed her away, he hoped she would stay.

Emma bit down on her bottom lip, taking a deep breath. She turned her face away from him. "I...I don't know how to even respond to that." Her voice shook as she watched Anna and Ben. They meshed so close to one another, it seemed impossible to tell where one ended and the other began.

Sean pushed his fingers through his hair. "I'm sorry that I've made a mess of everything." A long paused followed.

"It's fine... It was just a kiss." Emma shrugged. "Nothing to get all worked up about." She straightened. Stepping away from him, Emma ended whatever dangerous waters they were bound to float down by continuing to stand there. Her eyes flickered across his face, taunting him, drawing him in. He wished it had been just a kiss like all the ones before. But it wasn't to him because that single kiss was making him reevaluate everything. Glancing over her shoulder, her lips forming a small, tight smile, Emma told him to have a nice night, as she walked away.

"What? Wait." He chased after her, struggling to process the words he needed to say to make her stay. Quickly, Emma melted into the sea of people. He followed behind her, ducking and diving in and out of the crowd. Finally, a few feet from her and steps from the exit, he called out to her.

Emma whipped back around, staring at him. Emma's jaw clenched and eyes narrowed. "What?" Her voice was laced with irritation.

Sean slinked back as he failed to find the right words. He was at a loss. Impatient with him, Emma continued outside. He trailed behind her, joining her on the sidewalk.

The wintery air hit his skin, slicing through him. He popped up the collar of his sports coat, digging his hands deep into his pockets. He shuffled his feet to stay warm.

Why had he made a mess of everything? He longed to pull her near in an embrace, to feel the electric rush of her body against his. To run his fingers through the strands of her hair, while he whispered the ways in which he could make her happy, if she would only choose him. If only he could... or would. But he knew deep down he would fail. Fail like he had failed all those times before. He was a man who couldn't commit.

Emma ignored him. Her posture rigid. Digging around in her purse, she pulled out a pair of gloves and put them on. Then she wound her scarf around her neck, tugging it tight. Afterwards, she glanced up at him with a raised eyebrow.

Desperately, Sean wanted to change things, to right the path. "Can we be friends?" His voice came out as a desperate plea. "I can't stand knowing you hate me."

Emma rolled her eyes, throwing her hands up. "Don't be dramatic. I don't *hate* you."

Emma searched in her purse, pulling out her keys. She

glanced down the street, avoiding eye contact with him, she continued. "I barely know you, and we only shared a few dates. I'll see you later, Sean." She continued toward her car.

Sean jogged to catch up with her, reaching out he touched her arm. "Please." He pleaded. "I like being around you, Emma. You're important to me, and I hope we can be friends."

Emma halted in front of her car. He dropped his hand, cowering back a step.

She exhaled, pinching the bridge of her nose. "I don't kiss my friends."

"I know. I know. But..." He waved his hand. "What if I promised that it would never happen again?"

"What part?" Impatiently, she rubbed her hands together, shuffling her feet to stay warm.

"The kissing part..." Sean shifted on his foot, buttoning up his sports coat. "I promise to not kiss you again."

Emma paused, closing her eyes for a moment. "Let's be honest, that's never going to work." She waved her finger between the two. "It'll end up leaving both of us frustrated."

Sean nodded. "Yes, it could, but we could both use a friend right now."

Everything within him found it imperative he didn't lose her again. If she wouldn't date him, at least he could still be around her, as a friend. Did the plan have fatal flaws? Of course, but it was worth a shot. Some of Emma was better than none.

Lingering, Emma clicked the unlock button on her key. "I don't know... It will just create problems for both of us." Catching her gaze, Sean's middle warmed. His body awakened. The static air crackling between them.

Sean stepped toward her, resting his hand on the corner of the door. "Let's try. Plus, now our friends are friends. I'm sure we'll be thrown together again. Do we really want it to be awkward when we see each other?" He raised an eyebrow.

Exhaling, she gnawed on her bottom lip. "I should say no..." Her eyes darted up the street, way past him, back to the restaurant where their friends celebrated. Eventually, she turned back toward him.

Eyes locked, his skin burned, and every cell in his body bathed in the warmth of her unrestrained attention. "But say yes." He gulped. Their closeness, making his head spin like he was on a rollercoaster. "I promise. Just friends. Nothing more."

She slipped into the driver's seat as Sean moved his hand from the door.

"Fine." Emma reached out to shut the door. "You can call me next time you want to hang out *as friends*." Her voice lingered on the last two words. Quickly, she closed the door, and drove away.

* * *

Looking once in the rearview mirror, pulling away from the restaurant, Emma saw Sean remain on the sidewalk, watching her drive away. Once he was out of sight, she screamed in the empty car, slamming her hand down on the steering wheel in frustration.

Fingers stinging, she shook them vigorously. In one swift movement, she flipped on the radio. Anything to take her mind off tonight. Off Sean, and her undeniable attraction to him. He wanted to be friends? The thought made her blood simmer. Emma didn't want to be his friend. She wanted to date him. Kiss him. Cuddle up with him on the couch. Not to be his friend. That was why she had let him go. Who needed a friend when what they wanted was a boyfriend? Fiancé? Husband? Why had she agreed to this ludicrous plan?

The engagement party had drugged up some of her unresolved issues. Her feelings of rejection. Her longing to be part of a pair, a couple. Anna and Ben were so happy together. They had spent the entire evening in their own little love bubble. She had no doubt they would make it to the altar. Unlike herself.

What was wrong with her? Who was she anymore? Ashamed of the envy which coursed through her, Emma shook her head. This wasn't the person she wanted to be. Normally she was happy for others, not a raging jealous person. Mind muddled, she tried to redirect her thoughts. Anna was a good and dutiful friend and deserved every bit of joy directed her way. It was imperative that she be nothing but positive and supportive. To focus on her friend's successful engagement, not her complete and utter misery.

Exhaling, she counted out each second to calm herself down. Seeing Sean had rattled her. The world seemed determined to throw her a million curve balls. Emma resented how attracted she was to him. It was practically illegal for someone to look as good as he did. The man pranced on her weakened state. Clearly, he was able to shut down his romantic feelings for her or he never would've suggested being friends. Emma, on the other hand, couldn't get their kiss out of her mind. Or the effortless way they could talk to each other over the phone.

When he grabbed her hand, leading her to a quieter place, her heart raced faster than a racehorse. Once against the wall, only inches apart, his spicy cologne danced around her nostrils. The. Entire. Time. The smell severely impacted her judgement. The woman couldn't be held accountable for any of what happened afterwards. So, she had agreed to be friends. A horrible idea. Torture, really.

Aggressively, she flipped on her turn signal, pulling onto the highway. She bit down on her bottom hip so hard she tasted blood. His blue eyes taunted her with every turn. With all her might, she tried to act indifferent at the party, and not even look his way too often, because staring into his baby blues made her pulse quicken and temples throb. When it came to Sean, she had no defense.

The damage was done. Already, she was in far too deep. Caring this much so soon. Additional heartbreak was written over this entire scenario. Friends, she balked. This was never going to work. Rather than dwell on more of her serious lapse of discernment, she blasted her music and sang along the entire way home. Determined to stay as far away from Sean as humanly possible.

Chapter Thirteen

Her resolve only lasted a night. The next morning, a chime on her cell phone awoke her. Swiping at her eyes, she reached over, grabbing her phone from the nightstand. It took her eyes a minute to adjust to the light.

Sean: I have a house call out near Putnam State Forest. Would you like to tag along, friend?

Emma pulled back her covers, feet hitting the chilly wood floor. Rereading the text from Sean, making sure she read it correctly. The guy wasn't kidding when he said he wanted to be friends. Sunday dinner with her parents wasn't until five, so the entire day was before her.

Before she had time to think, her fingers skidded across her phone, typing her reply.

Emma: I have a family dinner with my parents at 5. What time are you doing this?

She tidied her bed while she waited for a reply, all the while knowing this was a mistake. Sean made her stomach flip and skin dance. Not touching him would be torture. But with all that, she wanted to see him again. His attention did something to her, buoyed up her spirit in a way no other guy had.

Sean: I'll have you back in plenty of time for your family dinner. Your house is on the way. I'll pick you up in a half hour. He didn't even wait for her reply. His boldness wasn't lost on her.

Emma reread the text and sent him her address. With only thirty minutes to look presentable, she ran to her bathroom to get ready. Since she didn't have time to do her hair, she pulled it up into a messy bun. Emma applied some makeup, then threw on jeans and a sweatshirt. Her outfit was something someone would wear to hang out with a friend, not a potential love interest. There was no use in letting the lines get blurred, at least for her. He wanted a friend, so she would be one. She flipped off her bathroom light as her doorbell rang.

The thought of Sean standing on the other side of the door made anxiety bubble up her chest. Her heart thundered in her ears.

Swiftly, she adjusted the tightness of the rubber band in her hair. Glancing in the mirror by the door, she double checked her makeup. She opened the door when she approved of her appearance.

"Sean." Her voice was more breathless than she would have liked. Emma caught his gaze, and she wondered if he liked what he saw. He smiled, his dazzling whites nearly blinding her.

"Emma…" He pushed his hands into his pants pockets. "Are you ready to go?

Pushing the door all the way open, she waved for him to step inside. "I need to find my boots and grab a coat. Come on in for a second."

"Sure." Sean stepped inside the small foyer, closing the door behind him. "Take your time."

He wore jeans and a thick corduroy jacket. *Man, he looked good*. Really good, like a cross between a cowboy and a hipster. Her nose picked up the same cologne from the night before.

The one which blurred her vision, making her head spin. *Focus*.

Emma reminded herself to concentrate, while she gathered her coat and boots from the hall closet.

As she tightened the last lace of her boot, she caught Sean watching her every move. His gaze made her skittish. With wobbly hands, she finished and stood.

She gulped. "How many house calls do you usually do? Is this typical for you?" She hoped her questions sounded casual.

"I don't know. Enough. But I'm one of the few vets who still do house calls, because of it I get a lot of extra business." He met her eyes.

Emma locked up and followed him out to his truck, where Sean held the door at its corner, waiting for her to climb in.

"Thanks." she managed, sliding into the truck.

The truck was old and rusty, but the inside was surprisingly clean. Being a bachelor for so long, she figured he probably lived like a slob. He climbed a full notch in her mind from the way he kept his truck tidy.

Sean opened his car door and got in next to her. The cab was tight and only a few inches were between them. Immediately, she was aware of the intimate feel of the cab, and Emma needed an invisible barrier where the lines of friendship and romance didn't become muddled.

Emma scooted as far over to her passenger side door as possible to keep from touching him. Practically sitting off the edge, the plastic from the car door poked into her arm.

Sean cleared his throat, breaking her train of thoughts. "It shouldn't take us that long to get there. Maybe fifteen minutes."

"Oh... okay." She shot him an awkward smile. Finding herself at a loss of a vocabulary of more than five words, her heart raced.

Starting the ignition, the radio came on blaring in the

background. The volume was high and overpowering. She jolted at the sound, covering her ears with her hands.

Sean fumbled around with the knobs, locating the volume, cranking it down. "I'm sorry about that." His cheeks burned a fiery red, his gaze meeting hers. His reaction was endearing. She guessed even the dreamy vet managed to get embarrassed now and then. "I think I bumped it getting into the car."

Their eyes locked again.

Emma's heart was in her throat, thinking of kissing him, so she turned her head away, forcing her gaze out the windshield. Studying the road, she attempted to keep her eyes off him. Sean made her swoon and stomach flutter like a baby bird taking its first flight. How she wished things were different, wished their script held an ending where they both got what they desired.

Sean flipped on the turn signal. "Thanks for coming with me." He pulled onto the road, driving at a slow and steady speed through her town. "This is such a serene drive, even in the winter. Come spring, it's simply beautiful."

Emma inhaled. Her nostrils flared as they picked up the scent of his cologne. It made her dizzy. Her eyes steady on the windshield, she replied, "I completely agree. It's very calm through these woods. It's why I love living out here."

He continued discussing the scenery, but Emma wasn't listening. Not when his arm was dangerously close to hers. Each thump in her chest became faster. All she could think about was kissing him. His lips on hers, but this time longer.

His words snapped her back to reality. "I'm glad I ran into you last night." Sean glanced at her, then back to the road.

Emma nodded slowly, biting down on her bottom lip. The words washed over her, seeping into her veins. He was glad he saw her. Did that possibly mean he wanted to kiss her, too? Wait, back up. The kissing wasn't the problem; it was his refusal to commit.

"It certainly surprised me." Emma glanced in his direction, trying to not study his chiseled jawline too carefully. "I mean... What are the odds we would end up with mutual friends?"

Sean chuckled. "Million in one."

He flashed her a bright smile, making her middle pool into a warm gooey mess. She remembered why she liked Sean, why she wanted to be around him. He had an ability to loosen her up, push away the tension, and remind her life wasn't always meant to be so serious. The only bright spots in the last months of her life had been with him in it.

Tapping his hand on the steering wheel, he asked, "Do you think Anna and Ben will be happy together?"

"Umm... Did we go to the same engagement party?" Emma raised an eyebrow, tilting her head toward him. "Those two were all over each other. They're perfect for one another."

Sean nodded slowly, smiling. "They did seem to be in their own little love bubble, didn't they?"

Emma faced him while his eyes stayed glued to the road. "They're in love. What did you expect?" She shrugged.

"I guess you're right... I imagine that's how all newly engaged couples act." He nudged her playfully with his shoulder. "Right?" He paused. His eyes flickered between Emma and the road.

Her arm warmed. Skin tingly, she focused on breathing, which was hard to do with him even closer than before. "I think if an engaged couple isn't acting like how Ben and Anna were acting... then the couple is bound to have some serious problems further down the road," added Emma.

Sean nodded in agreement.

A few silent beats of time and her breathing returned to normal. Her heartbeat slowed to its original pace. Emma said, "I'm not going to lie..." She wanted to divulge the words she tucked down deep inside, but wondered if Sean would think less of her.

"Come on, out with it, Emma. You can tell me." added Sean.

Emma took in the scenery they were passing by. Trees blanketed with white. Miles of snow as far as see could see.

Wringing her hands together, she said, "I'm not going to lie. It was difficult seeing Anna and Ben engaged and happy. I wish it hadn't been." She shook her head, wondering when things would be easier, when Jake wouldn't taint every part of her life, and when rejection wouldn't face her at every turn, making her feel unworthy of love. Her eyes found the lines in the middle of the road, and she kept her gaze steady on it. "I hate myself for not being entirely and completely thrilled for them."

Sean reached out, lightly grazing her arm. "It's okay," he assured her. "You're human, like the rest of us. Nobody faults you for that. I certainly don't. If anything, it makes me respect you more, because you recognize something in yourself you want to change." He gave her arm a quick squeeze, then gripped the steering wheel with both hands. "Promise me you won't hold back how you're really feeling. I want to be there for you."

Emma nodded, tears stinging the corner of her eyes. She looked away, not wanting him to see her all choked up.

Abruptly, Sean took a sharp left turn off the main road, pulling onto a single lane dirt road.

Emma hesitantly continued. "All of my friends are married now, and some even have kids." She fiddled with the ends of her large sweatshirt. "I never thought I'd be the last one." Her gaze went out the side window as thickly wooded trees lined both sides of the dirt road. "I never imagined I'd be the one forced to remain in the past while everyone else was moving forward." She exhaled, her shoulders drooping.

"I'm sure it's been rough."

Something made her divulge more, a comfort which she hadn't experienced with anyone else. "And... my parents are too much."

Sean smirked. "Really? How?"

"They mean well. I shouldn't complain. But if my mom looks at me one more time with that concerned look in her eyes, I might snap."

"I'm sorry. I'm sure it'll get better soon. At least they both care?" Sean reached out, patting her knee in comfort. "Don't worry, once you find the guy who's right for you, all of this will be a distant memory."

Emma's jaw clenched. "Where? Where am I going to meet this guy? If they're all like you, none of them will ever want to get married." Immediately, she regretted her words. She closed her eyes for a moment to regain her composure. "I apologize. That came out all wrong."

They jostled up and down in the cab as the road became bumpier. "No worries." Sean nodded. "But... Emma, don't give up hope. There are still guys who aren't like me. Ones who don't carry around the scars from a mess of a childhood." His voice faded while his expression became impassive.

Emma's heart plummeted. "I'm sorry for what you went through with your mom." She bit down on her bottom lip, searching for the right words. "And here I am complaining about how my parents care *too* much. I must sound like a real brat."

"No." Sean tightened his hands onto the steering wheel, maneuvering the rough drive. "You don't."

Emma gripped the door handle to keep from banging her head on the roof of the cab. The surrounding trees became thicker and denser. Her fingertips dug into the hard plastic. "Are you really a vet or a serial killer?" She joked.

Sean chuckled, quickly changing the mood. "I'm really a

vet. Promise. Not a serial killer. And we're almost there. It's a dairy farm. Trust me, you'll be able to smell it in about..." He glanced in his rear-view mirror then again peered at the road. "In five, four, three, two, one..."

Right as he said one, the farmhouse came into view, along with cows as far as the eye could see. The smell permeated through the windows. Emma pinched her nose in a fruitless attempt to block out the horrible smell. It was useless.

"You're right, I can smell them." Emma almost gagged.

"I told you." Smirking, Sean glanced over at her with taunting eyes. "You smell them before you see them." He pulled to a stop right as the road ended. A locked gate blocked the road that gave entrance to a barn house along with a pasture full of cows. "This shouldn't take too long. I've got to do a herd check."

Emma pulled opened her door and climbed out, slipping on her thicker jacket over her sweatshirt, while Sean reached into the bed of his truck. He pulled out a big vet bag.

"What's a herd check?" She pushed her hands into her pockets, regretting she hadn't brought gloves. The air nipped at her skin.

"A herd check is where I come to verify the cows' reproductive health, pregnancy, breeding. That type of thing. Believe it or not, these cows have a whole slew of people working to keep them producing milk on a regular basis." Sean pointed his head in the direction of the barn. "This way. They've a few pregnant cows they are worried about."

Emma fell into step next to him. The pungent smell tickled at her nose, forcing her to breathe through her mouth. "How do you get used to this smell?"

Sean snickered, his blue eyes flickering to hers. "You don't. It's awful. The worst part is our clothes will stink for the rest of the day."

Emma replied, "Perfect."

The flies swarmed around her, buzzing in her ears. She swatted them away. Wandering across the farm, they met the farmhand who had the pregnant cows lined up and sectioned off in a separate area.

Emma climbed onto the wooden railing, sitting on top. She watched Sean check each of the pregnant cows. Every cow he approached, he patted on the back gently, then rubbed slowly across their belly, before bending down to check for something. Her face flushed as she unabashedly watched him in awe.

Though the air was pungent, she breathed easier than she had in months. Being outdoors restored a part of her, lightened her spirit in a way nothing else had. Time ticked by as Sean worked on the cows, but Emma didn't mind. She had the entire day before her and was glad for the distraction. Maybe they could be friends? Maybe they could be friends who hang out together, and did things that friends did. Biting down on her bottom lip, she pushed the thought away because she wanted more. She wanted this Sean all the time.

Sean continued checking the animals, his shirt stretching across his broad shoulders, causing her to swoon. Try as she may, Emma couldn't keep from admiring him. He must have sensed her staring, because in the middle of her making googly eyes at him, he glanced up at her.

For a flicker of time, she swore she couldn't breathe. With only the thumping of her heart ringing in her ears, she gulped.

Sean pulled his attention away from her, bending down to reach under a cow. Her cheeks burned as hot as coals in a fire. Embarrassed, she jumped off the wooden fence. It was imperative she left, swiftly break whatever occurred between them. Distance was her only method of defense as everything bubbled up inside of her.

"I'm going to wander around for a minute." Her voice shook when she called out to him.

Sean peered up from where he was crouched down. His hands were covered in long gloves up to his elbows, covered in muck. "I'm almost done. Maybe like ten more minutes." He smiled, his dazzling blue ocean eyes taunting her.

For a moment, her mind went blank, like so blank she forgot how to speak, to carry on a conversation or make a coherent train of thought. She told him she'd be right back, her voice too high in a weak attempt to conceal how unglued he made her.

Briskly, she turned, walking along the well-worn path which hugged the pasture filled with cows. Only once Sean was completely out of sight did her breathing return to normal. Her pace slowing, she breathed in the crisp air. The sun was high in the sky, bringing some much-needed warmth, enough to bring some feeling back to her fingers. Lifting her face, Emma smiled as she bathed in sunlight. It seeped into her veins, pushing out the months of agony. Part of her was restored, maybe even healed. After she walked for a while, her temples no longer pulsating, she headed back in the direction she came.

Sean appeared on the path, calling her name with a wave.

Emma smiled. "All done?" Their eyes meeting, she stopped directly in front of him.

He pivoted on his foot to continue back to the barn. "Yep. All finished. I'll have to come back in a few days to recheck the same cows, but I think they should be just fine."

Their arms grazed one another as they walked. The touch was too much. Everything within her wanted to move closer, to reach for his hand, allowing her fingers to interlock with his, like they were a couple and not friends who were playing this silly dance where they both forgot the steps.

Neither said anything for a while. Emma was grateful for the solitude. It provided a moment to admire the woods and gather her racing thoughts. The barn finally peeked out in front of them. Sean broke the lull.

"Thanks for coming with me today. I need to bring you more often." He tilted his head toward her, their eyes meeting. His smile reached his eyes, making every flick of blue sparkle. "It made a Sunday house call way more enjoyable."

"You don't say." Her voice was too eager. She told herself to tone it down a notch, pulling her eyes away from him. "How so? I didn't even do anything except watch you poke and prod some cows."

Sean nudged her with his elbow as they neared his truck. "Yes, but I wasn't alone."

His reassurance made her ears ring and body buzz. She mattered to him. "Umm... I was happy to come." She stumbled over her words. Her skin tingled, and her heart rate was steadily rising.

"I'm glad you did." Reaching the truck, Sean swung his medical bag into the bed. He unlocked her door, holding it open for her. "I like being with you, Emma."

She gave a curt nod, while her heart nearly stopped. With wobbly legs, she managed to sit down on the truck bench. Once settled in her place, she glanced over at him.

Sean's gaze moved from her eyes to her mouth. Squeezing the corner door of the door with his hand, he lingered, then he looked down, grumbling. He closed the door and went around to the driver's side. This wasn't good. Mind a jumbled mess, Emma's resolve was quickly dissipating. Her temples pulsated when Sean slipped inside. He placed his keys in the ignition but didn't start the truck. Pausing, he turned to face her. His eyes flickered across her face, making her acutely aware of her appearance.

"Emma. Emma. Emma." He sharply inhaled. "What am I going to do? I like you too much."

She gulped, moistening her lips. "I don't know, but thanks

for inviting me." The words tumbled out of her mouth. The world around her became tipsy, with nowhere to land but in his arms.

He scooted closer, and she didn't move away. Instead, she boldly held his gaze. Reaching out, he tucked a few stray hairs behind her ears. Her heartbeat rang in her ears. She inhaled when he traced the outline of her jaw with a single finger, branding her skin as his touch left a blazing trail of heat that traveled down her spine.

This was a huge mistake. *Friends. Friends. Friends. He just wants to be friends! Be strong. Be. Strong.* It was useless. All she could think of was his lips on hers, dancing together.

Who leaned in first was a blur. Maybe it was him? Maybe it was her? But as soon as his lips glided over hers, Emma gave into him. The scent of his cologne danced to her nose, making her feel at ease. Tugging on his coat, she pulled him closer. Emma raked her fingers through his hair, massaging his temples. All the while, his lips dipped and dived over her own, making her forget every single kiss she had ever shared with anyone else. Ever. She embraced the moment, enjoying the exhilarating feel of his lips on her own. Finally, when reality struck, she quickly pulled away. Her hand flew to her heart as she willed her pulse to return to normal.

Blurting out, she exclaimed, "This was a mistake!" Emma buried her face in her hands as Sean cleared his throat.

"I didn't think it was a mistake." Emma peeked up from her hands, and Sean smirked. His hand roamed across her shoulders, rubbing back and forth in a hypnotic motion. "I think we both enjoyed it."

"You promised we would be friends." Emma's voice strained. "But nothing's changed. You never want to get married, and I do!"

The reality of their situation was suddenly in better focus. She and Sean could never be, and she didn't have the luxury of time. Maybe in her twenties, yes, but not now. She was edging too close to her expiration date. Time was ticking by way faster than she liked. Emma wanted children and a family.

He didn't protest or correct her. Instead, he glanced away, fidgeting with his keys hanging from the ignition. "True. I dare say we are at an impasse."

She scooted herself closer to the door, as far away from Sean as possible. The invisible physical barrier needed to be erected between them once more. If she didn't build it, nobody would, and her heart would fall deeper for him.

"I don't think we can hang out again." Her head was swimming, filled with the memory of his touch. "This was a bad idea." Emma glanced out the passenger window.

Sean considered her words. "I promised I wouldn't kiss you, and I did."

Her eyes darted to him. "See? We are two people who can never be friends."

"I know." He started the car, pulling out of the parking lot and onto the road. "You were right. We can't be friends." His words lingered in the air between them, creating a huge abyss so big no bridge could ever cross it.

Here she was, back at square one. A familiar narrative.

Enough.

No more Sean.

Time for something new. Tomorrow, she was signing herself up for one of those dating websites. She needed a distraction. Anything to take her mind off him, and the never could be.

Chapter Fourteen

Jaw clenched. Sean gripped the steering wheel. The rest of the car ride to Emma's house continued in palpable silence. Both knew it was the last time they would do anything together, and it was all his fault. Mistakenly, he believed he could resist her and be friends, when he knew she wanted and needed more. Obviously, he had messed everything up by kissing her. Who could blame him? Their chemistry was undeniable. It was unmatched to anything he had experienced before. If only he wasn't so tainted from the past, if only he believed in the future.

Pulling up in front of her building, the car barely at a stop, Emma opened her door, stumbling over her words.

He drank her in. All of her. The curves of her face, the reflection of the light across her hair, and the specks of green in her eyes. He wanted to remember it because, despite her beauty and grace, he refused to let go of his past and give into love. He hated himself all over again.

"It's okay," Sean muttered. "There's nothing left to say."

Emma gave a single nod, gnawing on her bottom lip. She pushed open the door all the way, jumping out. "Sean..." She lingered, her hand gripping the corner of the door like she was waiting for him to change his mind. To back track his life choices and admit he was wrong. When he remained silent, she swung her eyes away toward her apartment building. "I... I hope you have a nice day."

Sean gulped, his throat dry and scratchy. His stomach twisting. Failing in every way that mattered, he wished he was whole and healed. He wished more than anything he could rewrite his past, where he felt he was worthy of love. But the past is the past and, as much as one wants to forget it, sometimes it's impossible. Sometimes, some of us are too broken to be fixed. We let the chains of yesterday hold us down today.

"You too, Emma."

Emma shut the door, closing off the possibility of something great. His shoulders drooped as his chest clenched tight. He was an idiot.

Later that night, his dreams were a weird replay of their day. The kiss that changed everything for him played on repeat. Over and over all night long. It had some variation, but always ended the same. Finally, morning came.

The previous day and dream put him in a horrible mood. Clearly, he would never have what he desired, Emma. He threw himself into work because it was the one thing in his life he was still good at.

Sean slowly ran his hand over the belly of the poodle laying on his exam table. He glanced over at Mr. Greyson. "How long has Trixy been acting unusual?"

Mr. Greyson stepped closer to the exam table, rubbing Trixy in between the ears. "Maybe three days..." His voice trailed off. "I have to confess something."

Giving the dog one last pat, Sean picked up his clipboard from the edge of the exam table. He reviewed Trixy's chart, scanning the dog's past health history. "Go on."

"Trixy was playing out back and got caught in the fence.

The way I had to pull her out... she might have broken a bone or something. I feel awful."

Sean waved it off. "These things happen. Thanks for telling me. Now I know where to begin. I'll take Trixy into the next room to do an x-ray."

Mr. Greyson looked relieved. "I hope it isn't that, but Trixy hasn't wanted to move at all since then."

Sean leaned over the dog, gently picking up Trixy. "Go out to the waiting room. I'll be back to get you in a little while."

"Okay. Thanks." Mr. Greyson left for the waiting room.

The rest of the morning dragged by.

Along with the rest of the week.

And the next.

Secretly, he hoped Emma would text him. She didn't. He wondered if she missed him as much as he missed her. His phone remained silent. Apparently, he was the only one pining for something that could never be. Every free minute of his time was spent thinking of her.

After he was finishing up work on Friday evening, his phone rang.

"Dad. I'm glad you called," Sean answered. He reminded himself to be gracious and kind. "I haven't heard from you in a while."

Gathering his things, Sean walked through the clinic, flipping off lights with his free hand, while he juggled the phone with the other.

"Sean." Thomas enthusiastically replied. "It's good to hear your voice."

After he locked the door, Sean shoved his keys back into his pocket, climbing the stairs to his apartment. "It's nice to hear from you, too. How's Lisa? You still in marriage bliss?"

"She's doing great. Thanks for asking," replied Thomas.

"I'm happy to hear it." Sean settled onto his couch,

relaxing and slowly warming up to the idea of his dad getting married.

"I don't think this came up when Lisa and I came to visit you..."

Sean sat straight up. "What didn't you mention?"

"I met Lisa's children yesterday."

Sean's temples throbbed. "She has kids? How many? Why didn't you say anything?" He gripped his heart as its pace steadily rose. This couldn't be happening. His dad married was one thing, but stepchildren?

"You didn't exactly ask, and you didn't seem open to knowing more."

"That's not true." His tone was accusatory. Back peddling, he inhaled. "Okay... you might be right. You said kids... How many does Lisa have?" Sean willed himself to pull it together, to not say something he would regret.

"Three." Thomas stated, his voice upbeat.

"Three." He blurted out. "You've got to be kidding me. Next, you're going to tell me you're a grandpa," mumbled Sean.

"Actually, yes." Thomas chuckled. "I've got grandkids now. Five. Well, step-grandchildren."

"This can't be happening." Pinching the bridge of her nose, Sean closed his eyes. Forcing himself to exhale, Sean wondered when all the surprises would end.

His stomach churned. He was spiraling like a kid on a tilt-a-whirl ride with no way to get off. The writing on the wall was as clear as day. Thomas was moving on without him. Soon he would be left behind, when his mom had already abandoned him. He was alone, so utterly alone.

Why did everyone want to leave him? Was he that unlikeable? Desperately, he tried to focus as his dad rambled on about his stepchildren. Thomas gave him meaningless details he would never remember. These were the people who were replacing him.

Sean forced himself to listen.

"One is in New York and has two kids. The other two are in Connecticut. All three are married. Lisa already has five grandchildren. It's awesome." His voice was animated. Sean couldn't remember the last time his dad sounded enthusiast about anything.

"Wow. Imagine that." Sean cleared his throat, shifting in his seat. "Is there anything else I should know?" He forced an awkward laugh. "You keep hitting me with all these surprises. I don't know how many more I can take."

"Nah. That's it for now," said Thomas.

"Thank goodness." Sean laid back on the couch, willing himself to pull it together and not spin himself into a tizzy.

"I was mainly calling because it's going to be some time before I can visit you again."

"Okay..." Sean swallowed the words he wanted to say. The ones which would push his dad away forever. "No problem, dad."

"We have to split our time among all our children."

And so it began.

Our children.

Plural.

The thought permeated through his mind. *Ours. Ours. Ours. Not yours. Not you.* Everyone had a family, including his dad. Everyone but him.

"I understand. Thanks for calling." The sooner he ended the call, the better. Sean was skating at an exhilarating pace to the edge, and once he went over the cliff, he would be unable to hold back all the emotions trapped inside of him.

Sean hung up then chucked his phone across the room, making a loud bang as it skidded across the tile floor. Most likely, he had permanently damaged it, but he didn't care.

Nothing mattered anymore. Then he put his arm over his eyes and groaned loudly. He wanted to call Emma. She was the only person he wanted to talk to, the only one to whom he wanted to divulge his feeling of complete abandonment. If anyone would understand, it would be her.

* * *

Emma grabbed her lunch, heading to the classroom next door. She knocked on the door lightly. Anna glanced over her shoulder from where she was stapling some artwork onto her bulletin board.

"Hey, Anna. Do you have time to eat lunch with me today?" asked Emma.

Anna collected another of piece of artwork from a pile on the back credenza, stapling it next to the others. "I sure do. Come on in and sit down. I'm almost finished putting these up on the board, then I'll eat."

Emma took a seat at the back round table, pulling out her salad. Anna finished up and joined her with her lunch. The two chatted and ate, and eventually the subject of Anna's engagement party came up.

"Sean was there..." Emma wiped her face with her napkin. "The vet who doesn't want to get married."

Anna stopped eating mid-bite, eyes widening. "That was your Sean!" She set her sandwich back down on the table, brushing a few crumbles away.

Emma nodded. "He isn't mine, but yes. That's the guy." She pierced her fork on another piece of lettuce.

With a raised eyebrow, Anna gave her a sideways glance. "Why didn't you say anything earlier? My engagement party was weeks ago."

She shrugged, attempting to act indifferent, all the while

mentioning him made her blood simmer. "I wanted to, but it slipped my mind."

Lies, all lies. She hadn't stopped thinking about him or their kiss in the cab of his truck. The longing for what could never be was consuming her.

Anna pressed her palms flat against the table. "I guess he was Ben's friend from college." Then she waved her hand. "I didn't make the connection. Did you guys talk to each other at the party? What happened?"

"He came up to me." Emma avoided eye contact, staring at her salad. "We spoke for a while at your party. He said he wanted to be friends."

Anna tilted her head, giving her a pointed look. "We both know that will never work." She opened her bag of chips, popping one into her mouth.

Fidgeting with her fork, Emma glanced away, embarrassed. "I completely agree."

"What aren't you telling me?" asked Anna.

"We tried the friend thing." Emma folded and unfolded her napkin. "Let's just say it didn't last a day."

"What?" Anna practically spit out her chip.

"We ended up kissing in his truck." Emma took a swig of the soda, letting the fizz burn her throat. She tried to block out the memory of the two of them in the truck together. The kiss which trumped all kisses. "So, yes... I'm fully aware we can never be friends. It's impossible."

"You kissed... Again?" Anna's voice rose an octave. "When?"

"The day after your engagement party, he invited me to go on a house call to a cow farm out near my house. I don't know what happened. After I spent the morning watching him all gentle and calm with the animals, I couldn't resist."

"Geez." Anna shook her head. "Stop fighting it. Just date each other already."

Her jaw tightened, and she spoke through gritted teeth. "He never wants to get married. It will never work."

Slowly, Anna nodded. "That's right. Sean's an idiot."

A laugh escaped Emma's mouth. "We both can agree on that."

Anna chuckled, lightening the mood. Emma joined in, the tension in her chest loosening.

"I'm not hanging out with him again. I don't trust my judgement anymore." Emma pushed up her chin, straightening her back. "I even signed up for a dating website. Anything to get my mind off him. I filled out the dating profile and everything, but I can't bring myself to look at the matches yet. Do you think that's a terrible idea?"

Emma wondered how desperate she sounded.

"I think that's a great idea." Anna smiled encouragingly. "Just look at the matches. What do you have to lose?"

"Nothing?" asked Emma, sheepishly.

The bell rung for them to pick up their students from the playground. "I'm proud of you. You're trying your best to move on. It's a step in the right direction. Go with it," added Anna.

Emma wanted to believe Anna. Believe she was moving on, getting stronger. There was only one way forward. It was time she took the first step.

* * *

A few days later, Emma settled onto her sofa with a warm and fuzzy blanket. Clothed in her most comfortable pajamas, she was ready to watch a new documentary about the disappearing honeybees. Real earth-shattering stuff. Relaxing, she shoved popcorn into her mouth as she watched.

Her phone dinged. Pausing the show, she stopped eating and picked up her phone.

Sean: What are you doing? I must tell you the latest about my dad.

A few weeks had passed since their kiss, and neither had contacted each other. The man had some nerve. Anger seeped into Emma's veins. Right when she was ready to move on, he reeled her back in. Her palms sweated. Sean did something to her, making her feel out of control and defenseless to his good looks and charm.

Yesterday, she forced herself to scan through the online dating profile matches she received. Nobody stood out, and if anything, it left her more depressed. She was going to have to search the universe to find anyone halfway decent. Despite her want to throw in the towel, she wrote a few of the guys back. The ones who appeared to be the least sleazy of the bunch. Emma hoped there was a possible diamond in the rough.

Don't answer. Don't answer. Don't. Answer. Her resolve dissipated like the snow in spring.

Her fingers zipped across her screen without further thought.

Emma: What happened?

Interest piqued. Things had to be spiraling for Sean or he never would have texted her.

Sean: Apparently, I have stepsiblings. Now, my dad has stepchildren and grandchildren. Or does he? I really don't know how all of it works with step people.

Emma sat up on the couch, tucking her feet under herself. She tapped her top lip with her fingers as she mulled over how to respond.

Emma: Maybe this could be a nice surprise? More people to love.

She saw the three little dots dance around on the screen as she awaited his reply. Then they stopped. Immediately after, her phone rang. Her heartrate began a staccato beat while her cheeks warmed. *Bad Idea. Don't answer.*

"Emma?" The sound of his voice warmed her middle like a gooey brownie straight from the pan. Her heart fluttery, making her swoon like a teen on prom night.

"Hi." Emma adjusted the phone on her shoulder before she replied, her voice unsteady. "So... How many stepsiblings do you have?" She grabbed the empty popcorn bowl, wiggling from the couch. She took it to the kitchen sink.

"Three." His voice deflated like three were a thousand.

"Three. That's nothing." Her voice high and animated, a pathetic attempt to sound upbeat. "I'm sure they're fantastic."

"Maybe..." There was a long pause. "But I can feel it..." Another pause.

Lingering in the kitchen, she rinsed off the popcorn bowl and placed it in the dishwasher. "Feel what?" Emma asked.

Sean loudly exhaled. "My dad's moving on, and soon he'll be leaving me, too."

She strode back to the couch. Sitting, she pulled a blanket up over her shoulders. "I don't think it's possible for him to leave you. He might be moving forward yes, but you're no longer a little kid. It's the natural progression of life, but you'll always be his child. Nothing or anyone will ever change that."

"No. This is different..." His voice strained. "All those new stepsiblings are married and have kids. My dad was thrilled to be a part of all that *with* Lisa. I'm being left behind... I'm losing him."

She sighed, wondering if she should state the obvious. If Sean was open to the idea of marriage and having a family of his own, his focus would be on that and not this. "Do you want my advice?"

He groaned. "I'm not sure I do." Sean paused. "Fine... Out with it."

Emma gripped her phone tightly. "Okay..." she hesitated. "If you found someone, got married and started a family of your own, your dad and his new life wouldn't be impacting you in this way." She ran her fingers through her hair. "Your dad is creating something new for himself, but you could, too. You don't have to be alone, but you're choosing to be. So don't be. Go out and find your own happily ever after."

Dead silence. A shiver ran down her spine, because she knew she had pushed him too hard. If someone didn't help him see the flaws in his thinking, then his life was going to be a lonely one. Pulling the phone away from her ear, she double checked the connection. "You still there?"

"I'm still here," he mumbled. Clearing his throat, Sean stated, "I think what you are saying makes sense. I wish I were in a better place to take your advice, because I value your opinion."

Sean ended the phone call.

He might value her opinion, but it didn't mean he was going to change. She knew it as broad as daylight. Sean and her would never end up together. They wanted different things. Emma tossed her phone down on the couch cushion next to her. Instead of stewing over their random and brief conversation, she walked to the kitchen table and plopped herself down in front of her laptop, opening it up. With a few clicks, she had the dating website pulled up on the screen. A few more matches had been added, and she scanned through the profiles. One guy named Adam looked fine. No red flags screamed out at her. She was tired of waiting. Tired of wasting her time on guys who refused to commit or broke her heart. Typing up a quick message, she hit send.

Chapter Fifteen

Emma didn't hear from Sean again during the week. Or the next. Or next. Their so-called whatever it was ended, for good.

To keep her mind off her own loneliness, she spent the evenings communicating with potential dates on the new dating website. Adam, the first guy she had sent a message to, ghosted her after they exchanged messages for a week. Over the last two weeks, she had been communicating with a guy named Grant. She wanted to set up a date to meet him in person, but she didn't have the courage to do it alone.

The last day before spring break, Emma locked her classroom. Glancing over her shoulder, she spotted Anna exiting too.

"Are you as ready for spring break as me?" asked Emma.

Anna laughed. "Am I?"

Though she had no big trip planned, she was excited to spend the week sleeping and lounging around her apartment.

Tossing her keys into her purse, Anna juggled her bag full of children's books. "I had so many parent-teacher conferences this past week. I apologize that we haven't had time to talk."

Emma had been in the same boat. "No problem. I totally

understand. I've been busy, too." They walked in step through the hallway of the school out to the parking lot. "I've been meaning to ask you for a favor..." Her voice trailed off.

"Sure." Anna turned, eyeing her with a raised eyebrow. "What's the favor?"

Emma exhaled, embarrassed she needed to enlist the help of her friend to go out on a date. "The thing is... I met this guy online who I've been talking to for a few weeks. And..."

Before she finished, Anna interrupted, her voice animated. "Really? Go on..." She waved her hand for her to continue.

"I want to meet him in person, but I've never done online dating." Emma fiddled with her keys, darting her eyes away from Anna to the parking lot. "I'm a little nervous about meeting a stranger this way. I wanted to see if you and Ben could go on a double date with us?" Emma made the last few steps across the parking lot and arrived in front of her car.

"That's it." Anna laughed, shoving her playfully. "Of course! From your tone, I thought you were going to ask me to donate a kidney for you or something."

Shaking her head, Emma chuckled. The tension in her shoulders and neck loosening. "No, no, nothing like that."

Anna opened her passenger side door, setting her bag of books inside. Closing the door, she walked around to the driver's side. Emma trailed along behind her. "You let me know when and where, and we'll be there. I can be your wing girl. If it's going bad, Ben and I can make up an excuse for us all to leave."

Emma smiled. "Perfect." She walked the few feet over to her driver's side, opening the door. "Great. I'll see if we can meet this Saturday. If that works?"

"We're free." Anna as she slid into the driver's seat. "Just text me. Bye." She reached out to closed her door.

A feeling of hope entered her heart. Maybe Grant would turn out to be as great in person as he was through email and texts? Starting her car, Emma decided to take the long way home. Being spring, it gave her a chance to admire the new blossoms sprouting on every tree, plant, and bush. In a way, she believed it was a new beginning. Each day, she took a step away from the agony of the past. A little away from Jake. And Sean.

Later in the evening, when she was feeling brave, she texted Grant, asking if he wanted to meet in person on Saturday night. He enthusiastically replied yes.

* * *

Saturday night, Emma sat across the table from Ben and Anna in the local Italian restaurant.

The restaurant was slightly stuffy and overly crowded. Ben tugged at his shirt collar. "What does this guy look like?" He asked.

"I've got a picture." Emma dug her phone out of her purse and pulled up Grant's dating profile. Then she held it up for them to examine. "Here he is."

Anna grabbed the phone out of her hands to get a better look. "Nice. He's cute." She scrolled down and read a little of his profile. "It says here he's an avid hiker." She eyed her suspiciously. "When have you ever gone hiking?"

Emma snatched her phone back. "I've been hiking before."

"When?" Anna leaned her elbow on the table, cradling her chin.

Emma was irritated. So, she didn't like to hike? Big deal. Every relationship needed some compromise, right? Anna had no clue how difficult it was to find a man these days. How could she? She had been dating Ben for half a decade. Things had changed. Dramatically. The pickings were slim.

Emma stared down at Grant's profile again, reviewing his description. "I admit I haven't been hiking recently. Big deal."

Anna laughed. "Not recently. Ha. Try *never*." She cocked her head to the side and gave her a pointed look.

Ben's eyes darted between them. "The guy likes to hike. I don't see the problem." He wrapped his arm around Anna's shoulders, giving them a squeeze. "I'm sure if he loves it that much, he wouldn't expect Emma to go every single time he wants to hike. You can have different interests."

Emma pushed up her chin, pointing at him. "See? Ben gets it."

Anna rolled her eyes and nudged Ben. "Don't encourage her. A guy needs to fall in love with the real Emma."

"I think Emma's trying to have an open mind." Ben reached out and took a drink. "Right Emma?"

"Correct," Emma agreed.

"Give them a chance." Ben kissed Anna playfully on the temple. "You never know with these types of things."

Anna held her hands up in defeat. "I'm sure he'll be great."

Emma shifted in her seat, scanning the front of the restaurant. No sign of him. She turned back around. "You don't think he's standing me up, do you?" She pushed her sleeve, revealing her watch. He was only two minutes late.

"Nah." Ben waved his hand. "We were here a little early, remember?"

"I know." Emma's legs started to shake under the table, bobbing back and forth as nerves surged through her.

Anna reached across the table and gave her hand a squeeze. "Don't worry. He's coming."

"Thanks. I sure hope so." Emma mustered a weak smile. "I don't know if my heart can take being stood up."

Silence followed. Emma impulsively checked her watch again.

Finally, Anna spoke up, filling the void. "I never told you, Ben." Her eyes darted between the two of them. "Emma knows Sean. The old college friend of yours."

Inwardly, Emma groaned. Why Anna thought it was a good time to bring up Sean was a mystery to her. The mere sound of his name made her stomach clench tight.

Ben shifted forward in his seat. "You don't say. I'm seeing him next week. We're meeting up to see a basketball game at our old alma mater."

"Isn't that nice?" Emma added out of politeness, not out of the desire to hear more. "That should certainly be fun for the both of you."

"It'll be nice to catch up. Sean's a great guy." Ben reached over and took a sip of his water. "If things don't work out with you and Grant, maybe you should date Sean. I don't know why I didn't think to set the two of you up before."

"I was engaged to Jake, remember?" Emma added, trying with all her might not to let the bitterness of the last few months of her life seep back in.

Ben flashed his eyes at her. "That's right. I forgot about that guy. Enough about him." He waved him off. "How do you know Sean?"

Emma clutched her together hands tightly under the table. "We met when I went skiing. The ski trip that was supposed to be my honeymoon." Emma craned her neck back to the entrance. Luckily, she spotted Grant. Extra grateful her date had showed up just in time to squash their conversation. "I think he's here." Her heartbeat picked up its pace. She stood, smoothing out her shirt tucked into her black pencil skirt. "I'll be right back."

From where she was, Grant looked even better than in his pictures. She smiled to herself. Maybe this evening was going to go her way after all.

Chapter Sixteen

Sean grabbed his keys off his nightstand along with his wallet, shoving both into his pocket. Next, he grabbed a jacket out of the hallway closet. The grandfather clock in his living room chimed, he needed to hurry if he wanted to arrive on time. Quickly, he shot Ben a text to let him know he was on his way.

After an easy drive, he pulled into the parking lot. It was already crowded. He scanned the rows for an empty spot. He couldn't remember the last time he had visited his old college campus and was grateful Ben had invited him to go tonight. Finally locating a spot, he pulled in.

Over the past few weeks, his schedule had been packed with a variety of new and old clients. To avoid any down time, Sean had taken all requested house calls, no matter the time or day. Being home alone bothered him in way it hadn't before he met Emma. Though Sean wasn't super social, lately he had become a full-on recluse. Clearly, he was in a rut. He was hopeful tonight would help change his mood.

In the past, after a long week of working, he usually ventured out to bars or other social events in the hopes of meeting a woman to keep him company for as long as he found her interesting. Then, when things became too serious, he cut the cord and let her go. This vicious cycle had carried him through his twenties, then part of his thirties. Now his life choices seemed dismal. The process daunting, and not as appealing. He only wanted one woman, Emma.

After their last conversation, their contact had ended. The woman had firmly put him in his place by pointing out his fatal characteristic flaw. A flaw which had been his constant companion for years. The inability to commit. But who was he kidding? When he refused to text or call Emma, he had only hurt himself. He missed her. Honestly, he couldn't remember ever longing to be with someone the way he longed for her. The whole thing was driving him wild.

His alma mater was swarming with enthusiastic fans, who forced him to weave through the crowd in search of Ben. A few minutes prior, Ben had texted him, letting him know he was waiting at the entrance to the basketball arena. One more scan at the crowd, and he spotted him.

Sean waved as he walked toward him. "Ben, it's good to see you." He gave his friend a quick hug.

"You too. Can you believe how long it's been since we've gone to school here?" asked Ben.

The two walked over to the entrance line, inching their way forward toward the doors. "No. I can't. It seems like yesterday we were attending school here." Sean took in all the people surrounding him, mostly students. The students appeared way younger than he remembered looking, more carefree and jovial than he ever felt. His good ole' college days were now a blur. "The students here look like babies." He shook his head, wondering where the last fifteen years of his life had gone since graduation.

Ben laughed. "I know, right? I guess we looked like them too... once." Emphasis on the last word.

Sean scratched his head. "I find it hard to remember any of it or even how it felt to be young."

In line, they were directly behind some students who were laughing and joking with one another. A stark contrast to Sean's rather lonely life. These students were in the prime of their lives ready to face whatever life had in store for them. He wanted to tell them to enjoy it now, because it only goes downhill from here. Life's not all it's cracked up to be.

Ben eyed him. "We aren't young anymore, are we?"

"Nope." He mumbled. "I guess not." Reality hitting him like a ton of bricks. A huge amount of time had passed on by without him even recognizing it. His bachelorhood was now a lifestyle choice. A choice which didn't have the women swooning anymore. Maybe it worked in his twenties, but in his thirties? Nah, all the women he knew wanted to settle down.

The worker at the door scanned their tickets. After entering the arena, they found their seats. The game started, the noise making it too loud to talk. Both watched the game, cheering on whenever their team scored a basket. By half time his mood was significantly better. Getting out and being with Ben had lifted his spirit immensely. The cheerleaders ran onto the court to start their half time routine when Ben asked if Sean wanted something from the snack bar.

Sean agreed, stood up, and stretched. They wandered down to the snack bar, getting in line. It inched forward. Sean attempted to speak over the throng of people. "Not much longer till the wedding, right?" He shoved his hands in his pockets, looking at Ben.

Beaming, Ben said, "Only another month."

Sean remembered the date from the invitation he had received a few weeks prior. "Is it just me, or was your engagement incredibly fast?" Sean thought people stayed engaged for at least a year. He certainly would've needed more time.

"I've been with Anna for half a decade..." replied Ben.

Sean interrupted him. "Has it been that long?"

"Yes." Ben shuffled his feet as they moved forward in the line. "I know what I'm getting with Anna...and honestly, I'm glad the engagement has been fast. It has kept all the wedding preparations from getting out of hand, and besides, I would marry Anna tomorrow if I could."

Sean raised an eyebrow. "Are you that positive about this whole thing?" His voice was laced with skepticism.

"Yes. I'm positive. Anna is the one." He shook his finger at Sean. "You just wait till you find the right one, you'll be running to the altar to lock her down before someone else gets the chance."

"I highly doubt that," Sean mumbled.

"You'll see what I mean. I didn't believe I would be like this either, but here I am."

At the front of the line, the conversation was interrupted. Sean was relieved to discuss anything else besides getting married and finding the one. The thought made his heart race and hands clammy. They both ordered hot dogs and sodas, then made their way back to their seats. A few minutes remained until half time was over. Sean took a bite of his hot dog, then a swig of his soda.

Ben took a bite and wiped his face with a napkin. "I almost forgot... I didn't know we had a mutual friend... Emma, who works with Anna."

Sean was mid-sip of his soda and gulped it down. "Emma?" He nearly choked on her name. He coughed until the soda made it down his throat. "Sorry. Yes, Emma." He waited for Ben to elaborate.

"She's terrific. I've known her for a few years now. She mentioned you two were friends. According to her, you met while she was in Bluebird on a ski trip with her mom. A trip that was supposed to be her honeymoon." Ben waved the story off. "Anyway, last week Anna and I went on a double date with her and some guy."

Sean nearly dropped his soda. "You did what?" His jaw dropped.

Ben raised an eyebrow as he looked at Sean. "We went out to dinner with her and some guy she met from online dating." He casually took another bite of his hot dog, while Sean's pursed his lips together. "Why, are you interested in her or something?"

"No." Sean blurted out too forcefully. "Sorry... I was caught off guard. Last I heard, Emma was still mending her broken heart." Sweat gathered on his brow, and he swiped it away.

"No. Emma's ready to move on." Ben finished eating and leaned back in his chair. "Rightfully so. From what Anna has told me, her fiancé really did a number on her. She seems rather determined to not dwell on the past, and she wants to get back out there and find someone new."

Sean stopped listening and begrudgingly took another bite of his hot dog. His mind ran rampant with images of Emma in the arms of another man. A surge of jealousy raced through his veins faster than a shot of adrenaline. Emma, dating? He wanted to date her. Kiss her. Be with her. Not some other guy, but he held no claim on her. If anything, he was the bonehead in this whole scenario.

"Did it go okay?" His interest piqued, unable to resist asking. Secretly, he hoped it had crashed and burned.

"I think so." Ben added with eyes on the basketball court. The buzzer rang for the second half to begin. "Last I heard, they were dating exclusively." Those in the arena clapped as the team ran onto the court, and Ben rose to cheer.

In a daze from the revelation, Sean joined and aimlessly began to clap along with the others in attendance. His mind a thousand miles away. Emma. All he could think about was her, with another man, with his arm around her. Another man kissing her. His stomach soured.

The rest of the game passed in a nauseous haze. The guy was probably already in love with her, a real smitten kitten. There was no denying it. Emma was incredible. The other guy, no doubt, was far smarter than him. He probably wasn't afraid of commitment, willing to give Emma what she so rightfully deserved. The man was probably not held back from the scars of his past, but instead ready and willing to give into love. Sean was spiraling as he tortured himself with various scenarios of Emma with the other guy. The whole thing caused Sean's heart rate to rise to an astronomical level. For the first time, Sean wished he was capable of a real relationship.

Chapter Seventeen

In the bridal dressing room, Emma took Anna's wedding dress off the hanger and held it for her to step into it. Next, Anna put her arms through the sleeves, and Emma buttoned the intricate buttons lining the back of the lace fabric. It was a tedious process, but Emma reminded herself this was Anna's day. Not hers. Tenderly, she finished the last button.

The two friends locked eyes in the full-length mirror. Emma smiled back at Anna. Tears stung the corners of her eyes as they exchanged a moment of happiness.

Emma's wedding dress, the one she never got to use, hung in the corner of her closet. It was pushed back as far out of the way as possible. Sometimes when she dug around for a missing shirt or sweater, it poked out, reminding her, in case she had managed to forget. A sting of rejection from a man she had loved, but who never loved her back. One day she would be strong enough to take it off the hanger and throw it in the trash.

The smile stayed on her face. Maybe today wasn't her special day, but someday it would be. Grant was sitting in the chapel as her date. He thought she was special. Eventually, she might believe him. Did Grant make her stomach flip when she saw him? No, not yet. She hoped with time he would. Not everyone has the deep, knock you off your feet, love. Instead, some had to settle for the one they loved second best. Some had to grow into love. Emma believed she could grow to love Grant. On paper, he checked all the boxes.

"There." Emma gently patted the back of her dress then reached up, squeezing Anna's shoulders. "All done."

Twisting around to see the back of her dress, Anna admired her silhouette. "Perfect. I love it." A smile radiated across her face, warming Emma's heart.

Anna's mom entered the small changing room and brightly smiled. "You look beautiful." The mother and daughter embraced.

"Thanks," said Anna.

Next, Emma helped straighten her veil, making sure it hung perfectly behind her. Gathering their bouquets, she handed Anna hers. "You make the perfect bride. I'm so happy for you. Ben is one lucky guy."

Anna gave her a quick hug, squealing. "It's like a dream. I can't believe I'm getting married."

The wedding planner poked her head into the room, announcing it was time to line up and walk into the chapel. Everyone filed into place. The doors to the chapel swung open, and music spilled out. The tantalizing smell of roses lingered in the air as they lined the pews. Emma began the walk down the aisle, spotting Grant in a back row and smiled at him. She was relieved he had agreed to come as her date.

When she arrived at the front, Emma turned to face the pews. She spotted Sean almost immediately, and their eyes locked. His gaze made her skin tingle and her head spun, warmth gathering in her stomach. Emma wished the blush splashing her cheeks wasn't a dead giveaway of her romantic feelings for him.

For a few moments, neither broke their gaze. Unconsciously, she smoothed out her dress with her free hand, while the other held her small bouquet of flowers. His glance unnerved her, then infuriated her.

Pushing up her chin, she straightened her shoulders. Reminding herself Sean had his chance, and she had no plans to allow him to ruin her day or weaken her resolve. The wedding march began, breaking their stare. All turned their attention toward the back of the chapel once Anna entered and walked down the aisle.

Arriving at the front, Ben stepped next to Anna. Their fingers intertwined, their love captivating their guests. The pastor began to speak, but Emma heard none of it. Her mind was fixated on Sean. The steady rise of her heart rang in her ears, making it hard for her to concentrate on the ceremony. Her gaze flicked to his every so often, with Sean's never leaving Emma.

When the ceremony concluded, Ben and Anna walked together down the aisle to the outside of the church, with Emma and the rest of their wedding party following them. She refused to look at Sean as she walked by, holding her ground.

All the guested filed out of the church, spilling onto the crowded walkway. She waved to Grant when she found him in the crowd, and he joined her.

"I'm glad you came," Emma told him.

Grant pulled her close, kissing her lightly on her cheek, his eyes twinkling. "Thanks for inviting me."

Her mind danced to Sean, wondering if he saw them embrace. Was he jealous she was here with Grant? Fighting the urge to look for him, she forced herself to concentrate on Grant, who leaned in and told her how beautiful he thought she looked.

"You might have out staged the bride," he added.

The attention embarrassed her as her cheeks warmed from his compliment. She hit him playfully on the arm.

"Impossible. Anna looked amazing as a bride."

They linked an arm around each other's waist and followed guests to the reception.

Grant leaned in again, his voice low. "Anna looked great, but you are the most beautiful woman here."

Emma paused, turning her face toward him with a weak smile. "Thanks." She managed.

Grant did have a way with words, but part of her wondered if he was just a smooth talker, a man who had learned the tricks of the trade in wooing women. Though she was flattered by his attention, all she wanted to know was if Sean thought she looked beautiful. He was somewhere in the crowd.

Lights were strung overhead in the reception area, filling the space with a lovely glow. Delicate flower centerpieces were intricately placed on the tables as music played softly from the band. The whole ambiance created an aura of love. Scanning the tables for their names, they found their proper table and settled into their seats.

Emma still hadn't seen Sean. Maybe he had left? Or maybe he planned on ignoring her the entire night? Then again, perhaps he was here with someone else? She and Grant made small talk with the other guests at their table. An announcement was made that dinner would be served shortly. Then, out of nowhere, breathless, Sean slipped into the seat next to her.

Gaping, her eyes widened. "What are you doing here?" Emma hissed in a whisper.

Sean locked his gaze on the others at the table, not at her. He kept his voice low. "What do you mean? I'm here for Anna and Ben's wedding reception."

Adjusting his seat closer to the table, Sean ignored her and smiled brightly at the other guests. He introduced himself to everyone at the table, shaking hands with some.

Once he settled back into his seat, Emma muttered, "You aren't supposed to be seated next to me. I have a date. Anna would never do that to me."

Sean didn't turn his head, but kept his eyes directed toward the stage. The band had stopped playing, and someone on the stage started talking. Sean patted her thigh quickly under the thick tablecloth.

"Don't worry. I paid the guy who was sitting here twenty bucks to switch seats with me." Sean boldly met her gaze, smirking.

Head spinning, she narrowed her eyes. "Why would you do that?"

Sean was interrupted by the clapping crowd. Emma missed the announcement, but she clapped along with everyone else. The person at the mic droned on, but she heard no sound. She craned her neck to look in the direction everyone else was looking. All erupted into applause as Ben and Anna made their first entrance as husband and wife.

"You didn't answer me," Emma stated, squeezing her shaking hands together under the table.

"Because I wanted..." Sean shifted in his seat then adjusted his jacket. "I *needed* to talk to you." He reached for a glass of water and took a sip, as if he hadn't just caused Emma's heart to burst.

Emma folded her arms protectively, watching the person giving a speech. "I have nothing to say to you."

The announcements stopped, and the reception filled with the hum of conversation again. Emma reached out with a wobbly hand, drinking from the long-stemmed glass. The liquid burned her throat. The world spun off its axis, and she gripped the table with both hands. Why was Sean doing this? He was determined to ruin her evening.

Interrupting her rapidly racing thoughts, Sean reached across her place setting with an outstretched hand to Grant. "I'm Sean. I don't think we've met." He smiled.

Grant took his hand, politely shaking it. "Grant. I'm here with Emma." Wrapping his arm around her shoulders, he gave them a slight squeeze.

Emma remained frozen. Mind blank.

"That's wonderful." Sean reached out and grabbed the breadbasket. Taking a roll, he placed one on his plate and held the basket out to Emma. "Bread?"

Forcefully, she snagged the basket from him, almost making the rolls tumble out. Her eyes rolled up to his, scanning them. They twinkled back at her mischievously. This wasn't good. Sean had something up his sleeve, she could feel it.

After placing a roll on her plate, she passed the basket to Grant. He took one and passed it along. She mumbled under her breath, "I don't know what your angle is, but you better behave."

For three thumps of her heart, she maintained his gaze. He grinned and buttered his roll, taking a big bite. Emma huffed, glancing away. Her stomach clenched as her jaw locked. Tonight wasn't going to end well.

Casually, Sean leaned toward Emma and Grant. "Grant, how did you and Emma meet?" He popped another piece of his roll into his mouth.

Grant smiled at Emma, reaching to hold her hand. "We met online."

Emma caught Grant's eye and smiled tightly. Tearing at the roll, she shoved a piece into her mouth. The bread tasted like cardboard, but she chewed very slowly and forced herself to swallow. Sitting in between the two men made her heart fluttery and hands shaky. Why did Sean's very presence make the world tipsy and unsteady?

Sean smirked. "You don't say. I've never done online dating, but I've heard lots of people have had success meeting someone online." He smugly glanced back at her.

She narrowed her eyes. His cockiness and minor dig weren't lost on her. It irked her to no end. Who did this guy think he was? The man had his chance. The least he could do was leave her and her date alone.

Grant remained undeterred. "Without online dating, I'd never have met Emma, and she's incredible. Personally, I would say it's been a great way to meet people. Am I right, Emma?"

She tried to mirror his enthusiasm. "Of course."

"Emma *is* incredible." Sean rested his elbow on the table, cradling his chin. "You probably don't know this, but we're old friends. We go way back."

Caught off guard from his revelation, she choked on her sip of water. Nearly spitting it out. "Excuse me." She wiped her mouth with her napkin.

Interrupting their conversation, the servers appeared and placed the fish entrée in front of each of them. The smell of fishy lemon and butter made her stomach rancid. Taking a deep breath, she forced herself to remain calm.

Grant didn't let Sean's comment slide. After he took a bite of his fish, he asked, "Old friends, huh?" Grant's eyes darted back and forth between Sean and Emma. "How do you two know each other?"

She picked up her fork and knife, aggressively cutting into her fish. "I wouldn't say *old* friends. Just friends."

"Emma." Sean gave her a sideways glance. "We are old friends."

"Okay, friends..." Grant cut into his potatoes. "Again... how do you know each other? From where?"

"We have a mutual friend." Her jaw clenched, and she willed herself to sound undeterred. "It's not a big deal."

Sean paused. "Don't listen to her." He unflinchingly kept his attention on her while he spoke. "It's kind of a funny story. I'm sure Emma has told you about it, but I helped her when she got stuck skiing on the trip that was supposed to be her honeymoon."

Emma's jaw dropped. She had only started dating Grant, and she hadn't found a way to tell him about her failed engagement. A major oversight, yes, but she planned on telling him soon. Little did she know, Sean single handily desired to railroad her.

Grant stopped mid-bite, setting his fork back down on his plate. "You were engaged?" His voice was loud enough to distract others at the table, who now stared at Grant. "When? How long ago did this happen?" His eyes were wild.

Inhaling, Emma closed her eyes. This couldn't be happening. This evening was unraveling because of Sean. He seemed determined to ruin whatever she had started with Grant. Head throbbing, she found it hard to concentrate on anything except how much she hated Sean.

Chapter Eighteen

Sean was being a complete jerk. He knew it, but he couldn't stop. Seeing Emma with Grant made the green-eyed monster appear. Some part of him found it necessary to blurt out about her broken engagement, which was not his business to tell.

Grant needed to know. Emma was fragile. Her heart was tender. If he didn't treat her kindly, the woman would be left shattered. Until now, Sean hadn't realized how much he wanted to be the man to protect her. Hold her. Kiss her. Perhaps marry her?

Seeing her again, Sean believed he was the right guy for Emma. Before the thought of being married made him want to run for the hills. Not tonight. During the wedding ceremony, he couldn't stop staring at Emma or keep from thinking how beautiful she would look on *their* wedding day. Whoa, back up. Their wedding day? It was out of left field. He waited for his stomach to clench, for the feeling of fear to overtake him, but he remained eerily calm as a Sunday morning.

Emma's response snapped him back to the conversation.

"Yes. I was engaged." Her words were slow, like each word stung as it came out of her mouth.

Turning her back to him, she boxed Sean out. The three-way conversation became a two-way. He mindlessly ate more of his meal, but strained to eavesdrop on the rest of their conversation.

"You were engaged!" Grant repeated, almost shouting. "And you didn't think to tell me. What else haven't you told me?! What else are you hiding?"

Emma reached for his hand, but he snatched it away. "I was going to tell you. Promise. I just didn't have the chance." She pleaded. "It's not a big deal. Trust me."

The other guests at the table remained quiet, staring on as they watched the lover's quarrel with wide eyes.

Grant threw his napkin onto his plate and stood. "I don't even know you."

Emma chased after him as soon as he stormed off, assuring him she could explain.

Suddenly with Emma and Grant gone, he had the full attention of those at his table. Sean tugged at his shirt collar. The fabric felt rough and restrictive. Sweat formed on his brow.

"They'll figure it out." He waved it off. "This is a wedding." Sean held up his glass in a gesture for a toast. "To Ben and Anna."

All the members of the table picked up their glasses, slightly confused, but joined in. They returned to their own conversations after the toast, but Sean tried to see where Emma and Grant went. The announcer came back on the stage to announce the cutting of the cake, and the bride and groom's first dance. Shifting in his chair, Sean turned to get a better view as Ben and Anna made their way over arm and arm to the cake.

As they fed each other, Emma sat back down with a huff.

Her hair had loosened from its tight style, and her cheeks were flushed red. Glaring at him, she snapped, "I hope you're happy." Dramatically, she folded her arms.

Sean put his hands up. "What did I do?" He faked innocence.

Slinking down in her chair, Emma looked defeated. "You've ruined everything."

Everyone around them applauded as Ben and Anna made their way to the dance floor.

"I'm sure he'll get over it."

"I'm not counting on it," mumbled Emma.

The music started to play loudly. He wanted to continue their conversation and apologize, but it was too loud with the music blaring.

He closed his mouth, moving his gaze back to Ben and Anna as they shared their first dance. Somehow, he had managed to mess everything up further, and now Emma refused to even look in his direction.

The dance ended and people joined the newlyweds on the dance floor. Meanwhile, Emma and Sean sat in insufferable silence. It made his skin crawl with discomfort, because he hadn't meant to hurt her. Really, he hadn't. Simply put, he wanted to be the one with his arm around Emma. Not Grant. Maybe it was the love in the air, but he was fixated on the idea of being married to Emma.

Briskly, he stood, buttoning his top suit jacket button. Emma's eyes tracked him. It was time he took matters into his own hands before he chickened out. His life was full of regrets. He didn't want this night to be another one.

With an outstretched hand, he asked Emma for a dance.

She squirmed in her seat, rolling her eyes. "You've got to be kidding me. I'm not going to dance with you." Each word oozed hatred.

He shook his outstretched hand again, not willing to give

up. Not with this fire under him. Foolishly, he had pushed Emma away, and all of that was about to change. Tonight was the night he grew up. It was the first time he wasn't going to let the scars of the past hold him back.

He softened his tone, hoping to convey his sincerity. "Please dance with me. We're old friends, right?"

Emma glanced up at him, her eyes reflecting the lights strung above. His breath caught in his chest, middle filling with warmth. Never did a woman look more beautiful than Emma under the sparkly lights with the moon and stars above.

"Is that what we are? Old friends?" Her gaze bore into his, making him dizzy.

This time, he bent down in front of her, inches from her face. Time froze. Eyes locked. The air thick between them, practically pulsating with their unspoken, but clearly mutual, desire. "You know that I wish we were more."

Emma gulped. "And whose fault is it that we aren't?"

"Mine. It's all mine." He hoped each word conveyed what he had failed to realize before. "Emma, just one dance."

"Fine." Emma stood, pointing one finger at his chest, pressing it firmly into his shirt. "But only one song."

He caught a whiff of her intoxicating perfume. It made his head spin and body ache with a craving to hold her close. "I'll take whatever I can get." Sean meant it because any moment with Emma in it was better than none.

He reached for her hand, fingers intertwining, and he led her to the dance floor. With the throngs of people dancing, he dipped and dived through the guests. Emma tightened her fingers around his. The steady uptick of his heart made him wonder if this was the beginning of something new and different.

After he reached a far corner of the dance floor, a place quiet enough and away from the crowd, the music changed from an upbeat song to a slow song.

"Perfect," mumbled Emma.

She released her hand from his.

He spoke softly. "It's okay. I promise to behave."

Emma gave a curt nod. "I'm holding you to that." His hand found hers once more, the other rested around her waist.

The gentle melody played, and they swayed to the music. Eventually, Emma's body softened, and she leaned her head on his shoulder. He closed his eyes, holding on to the feeling of her in his arms. Blissfully, he tried to memorize the satin feel of her skin against his. The sweet scent cascading off her hair made the world topsy-turvy. He tried to remember all of her, all of it, because for a minute he wasn't scared to give into love.

"How many times are we going to do this with one another?" Emma slightly loosened her grip around his waist, tilting her head up toward him.

Dazed, his gaze washed across the soft curves of her face. "Dance?"

She blinked, staring into his soul, seeing through the facade he conveyed to the rest of the world. The world which no longer held the appeal it had just yesterday. In Emma's arms, he imagined a different, fuller version of life.

She shook her head, glancing away. "No, not dance... Denying what could be." Her gaze made his temples throb, mounting pressure in his chest. Every part of him craved her. He studied her lips, remembering how it felt to kiss her. Kisses which made him question everything.

"I... don't..." He struggled to find the words.

The song ended, changing back to a fast dance. The moment blew out like the leaves in the fall and, like a moron, he failed to pull it back.

"Never mind." Emma quickly let go, taking a step back from him. Wringing her hands, she added, "Thanks for the dance."

She left before he had time to respond, to say the words he needed to speak to make her stay.

Downtrodden, he wandered back to his table, settling back into his seat. Emma never returned.

The evening wrapped up. All the guests received sparklers as they filed out to the parking lot in anticipation of watching Anna and Ben leave. Holding the sparkler in his hand, he scanned the crowd one last time. A last-ditch effort to find Emma. His Hail-Mary pass. A laugh jolted him, and he turned in the direction, craning his neck in search of the woman that made him question everything. Her laugh, one permanently engrained into his psyche, led his way.

Sean waded through the crowd toward the sound of her voice. Finally, he landed directly across the path from her. She was laughing and holding a sparkler. The light from above beamed, illuminating her in radiant glow. Mid-laugh, she stopped, noticing him on the other side. They locked eyes. His throat was as dry as a bone, so he forced himself to swallow.

Anna and Ben passed by in the space between them. The crowd erupted into cheers. With all the surrounding noise, Sean heard no sound, only the trusty companion of his heart. After the happy couple continued to their decorated vehicle, he took a step toward her. Emma stood still. The sparkler still burning in his hand, her eyes followed him. Temples pulsating, he took another step of faith toward the woman he wanted to be his.

The others began to dissipate, but Sean kept his gaze firmly on her as he strode toward her. Inches from one another, he extended his hand, interlocking his fingers with hers.

Voice shaky, he said, "Hi."

Emma gulped. "Hi."

"I thought you left," he stated, resisting the urge to sweep a few stray hairs from her eyes.

The light around them faded and their sparklers burned out. Sean lightly tugged her closer. His eyes slowly adjusted to the darkness. "I thought I had blown it, that I'd lost my chance... Again."

A flicker of understanding flashed across her face. "You do seem to hold some sort of record." Emma teased.

"I know." Sean bit down on his bottom lip, wishing he had been different from the beginning. "I'm sorry."

Emma rubbed her temple, pushing up her chin. "Well... I don't forgive you."

Unable to resist, he tucked her loosened strands of hair behind her ear. "Yes, you do," he whispered. His hand glided down her body, stopping at the small of her back.

Lightly, she hit him on the arm. "No, I don't." The words didn't mirror her movements. She rested her hand on his chest.

He tightened his embrace around her waist. Leaning in, he spoke into her hair. "Liar." The word danced between them, casting its familiar net, pulling them closer, instead of apart.

A flicker of acknowledgement flashed across her eyes. She moistened her lips.

"I know," Sean cupped her cheek in his hand, his eyes searching hers, "because, if you were still mad at me, you wouldn't let me do this." He lowered his mouth to hers, reveling in their kiss.

Head twirling, his thumb traced the gentle glide of her jawline. Gripping him tighter, she melted against his chest. The feeling freeing and exhilarating. Holding her upright, he supported her weight as she twisted his hair around her fingertips. The air filled with her sweet tantalizing aroma. He was willing to give whatever she wanted to take.

In that moment, with Emma in his arms, kissing her, he swore he was transported elsewhere. They were in a world where he was no longer afraid. A man fully restored. No longer scared of the power of love.

His lips tingled and buzzed from touching hers. Finally, he forced himself to pull away. Breathless, he took her face into both of his hands, touching his forehead to hers as their breathing slowed.

Once his head stopped spinning, Sean glanced around the empty parking. They were the only two who remained.

Fidgeting with the lapel of his suit jacket, Emma's gaze fluttered up to his. "Please, Sean, don't make me regret this," she whispered.

The words made his middle warm.

Sweeping the outline of her jaw with his thumb, he replied, "I won't. I promise."

The words danced around them, reminding him of who he could be with her. The promise, one he didn't make in vain, laced them together. He had changed. This time was different. Emma had transformed him. Every part of him wanted forever with her.

Chapter Nineteen

Driving home from the wedding, Emma considered the evening. Sean was back, after ruining Emma's date and chasing off Grant. Why couldn't she resist Sean? He promised he wouldn't make Emma regret it, but had he really changed?

Parking her car, Emma wondered why she thought she could ignore Sean, even with Grant as her date. Then there was the kissing. Kissing him made her forget everything, especially her need to be levelheaded.

Exhausted, she wandered into her apartment, dumping her purse and all its contents onto her bed. Sighing, she pulled off her high heels, a welcome relief. Once changed, she settled into her bed. Before turning off her light, she grabbed her phone from the pile dumped onto the corner of her bed to plug it in. With all her bridesmaid's duties, she hadn't had a chance to check it.

She gasped. Numerous missed calls, and a slew of text messages from Grant lit up her screen. Quickly, she scanned through the string of texts. He apologized for storming off. A pit in her stomach formed. Grant had no clue she spent the rest of the night pinning for Sean, then kissing him. With no energy left to face the mess she made, she reached out and flipped off the light, immediately falling asleep.

Several hours later, she woke from a deep and dreamless sleep to the ringing of her phone. Her throat dry, mind muddled, she fumbled around for her phone. Without looking, she clicked accept. "Hello?" She flipped to her side, pulling back the covers of her bed.

"Emma. It's Grant." His voice was laced with irritation. "Why didn't you call me back?"

Emma sat straight up, running her hand down the length of her face. Her mind instantly cleared. "I didn't get home until late last night. I was exhausted and fell asleep almost immediately."

He sighed, clearly frustrated. "I called you twice and texted you a ton."

"I know." It was all she could muster. She didn't have the energy or desire to rehash everything with him. Grant was the one who had overreacted when he found out she had been engaged. If anyone should be apologizing, it was him, not her.

"I'm really sorry." His voice softened. "I shouldn't have stormed off like I did."

"No, you shouldn't have." She leaned forward, putting her head into her hands. Grant was a nice guy, but she kissed Sean last night. He was the one who made her head spin and stomach flip, not Grant. Even with all she knew about Sean, if it was a coin toss between the two, she would pick him. Idiotic? Yes. Bad judgement? Probably. Would she regret this all later? Highly likely.

"You've got to forgive me." Grant pleaded. "Give me another chance. I really like you."

"Look..." She paused, standing to pace back and forth. "You're a great guy. It's been nice getting to know you..."

"Stop." He interrupted her. "Please, don't go on. I know what you are going to say."

Emma raised an eyebrow. "What am I going to say?" Her fingers lifting to her hair, she pulled out the bobby pins she failed to remove the night before.

"That it's time we ended things."

A beat of silence communicated everything, until Emma could finally speak. "I think it's for the best." She pinched the bridge of her nose.

The image of Sean, his lips against hers, solidified her choice.

"It's that other guy, right? The one from last night?" asked Grant. "The one who is your so-called friend."

She closed her eyes and took a deep breath. "It doesn't matter at this point, does it?"

"I was right." He sighed. "I saw the way he looked at you."

"And how did he look at me?" Emma asked.

"Like you were the only one in the room." The words shot straight to her heart. Silence, followed, palpable, making her skin itchy. "Bye Emma."

Removing the phone from her ear, she stared down at the screen. Instead of feeling relief, anger seeped into her veins. Anger with herself, because Sean was her weakness, and so potent, she failed to think rationally. Nothing had changed from the last time they spoke. He would never commit.

With phone still in hand, she scrolled through her text threads, locating the one she had with Sean, one she should've deleted but never could. She typed rapidly into her phone.

Emma: I hope you're happy. Grant and I are finished, and now I've got to go to dinner at my parents' house, alone.

Jaw locked, angrily, she hit send.

Before she had a chance to jump into the shower, her phone binged.

Sean: Can't lie. I'm happy because I want to date you.

Emma didn't type a response. Date her? Here she was full

circle, right back where she was weeks ago. How about maybe marry her someday? Impossible, because the man didn't believe in marriage. Sure, he could say all the right things, but it didn't change that they wanted totally different lives.

Yeah, they had exchanged some incredible kisses that blurred her vision and caused her rational self to run for the hills. But, when all this hot and heavy stuff blew over, and Sean failed once again to commit to anything real, Emma would end up doing a 360. Only this time, she would be alone, depressed, and more frustrated than ever.

This had to end. Her fingers flew over her phone screen.

Emma: I only date people who want to get married someday.

He didn't respond. Surprise, surprise.

With nothing left to do, she stomped her way to the bathroom to ready herself for dinner at her parents.

A few hours later, she pulled into her parent's driveway. Grumbling, she slammed her car door. Her parents were expecting her to come with Grant. It was a rooky move. Next time, if there ever was a guy she was serious about, she wasn't going to introduce them to her parents until there was a ring on her finger.

Slugging her purse over her shoulder, she ventured into her parent's house. Hearing more chatter than usual in the kitchen, she wondered what was going on.

"Mom, Dad? I'm here." She yelled down the hallway toward the kitchen.

Melanie poked her head into the hallway, waving her over. "Come on in here, honey. Sean's already here." She grinned at Emma, causing Emma's knees to wobble.

She stopped right in her tracks. Was this a joke? How did he even know where her parents lived? She gave Melanie a wide-eyed look. Her eyes dilated. "What do you mean?" She hissed, nearly hysterical.

"Sean's here." Melanie smiled again. When Emma failed to mirror it, she tilted her head to the side, studying her face. "Why? What's wrong?" She closed the gap in the hallway between them. "Sean told us all about how you and Grant broke up last night. With you two being friends and all, he offered to come in his place. He didn't want you to be alone on such a tough day."

Her temples throbbed. The world around her twisting and twirling like she was on a carousel. "Unbelievable." Emma almost choked on her own words. "He has some nerve to show up here uninvited, and he thought it was his duty to tell you all about me and Grant."

Her nostrils flared. He knew he could never commit to her and knew of her attraction to him. This was a real low for him to push his way in when he should be fading into the background.

"You two are friends still, right?" Melanie put her hand on her hip. "He said you sat at the same table last night at the wedding." She inched closer to her daughter and whispered, "Am I missing something here?"

Emma lowered her voice to match hers. "How did he even know where you guys lived?"

"He called me this morning." Melanie glanced over her shoulder, checking to see if they were still alone.

Emma bit down on her bottom lip, with no idea how to remedy the situation. "How did he have your number?"

"We exchanged numbers at the hospital." Melanie threw her hands up. "I don't see what all the fuss is about. You did break up with Grant last night, didn't you?" She raised an eyebrow.

Emma ran her fingers through her hair, slowly nodding. "I did." Her voice strained. Inhaling, she closed her eyes to maintain composure.

"So, what's the big deal?" Melanie dropped her hands down at her side.

Emma wanted to scream. "Whatever." She mumbled.

Brushing past Melanie, she walked toward the laughter in the living room. Entering, she found her dad and Sean seated on opposite couches facing each other. Both glanced up as she entered. Brightly, Sean smiled at her, making his eyes twinkle their annoyingly perfect blue. Confused about his intentions, her lips formed a straight line. His eyes bore into hers, making her skin tingly and warm. Her tough exterior weakened by the second.

"Emma, I'm glad you made it." Noah pointed toward Sean. "I was just getting to know Sean."

"Is that so?" She fumbled over the words, avoiding further eye contact with Sean.

Noah pushed off the couch, standing. "I think the food is ready. We can all finish talking in the dining room."

Sean followed suit, standing. "It smells delicious. Thank you for having me." He flashed a smile at Melanie, who lingered between the living room and dining room.

Smiling, Melanie waved it off. "Anytime." Her voice was as sweet as cotton candy.

Noah and Melanie walked ahead toward the direction of the dining room. Sean attempted to follow behind them, but Emma firmly tugged him back by the sleeve of his shirt.

Clearing her throat, she announced, "You two go ahead." She forced a smile directly at her parents. "I need to talk to Sean really quick."

"No problem," replied Noah, as he and Melanie continued into the dining room.

Once out of earshot, she hissed, "What are you doing here?"

Sean wrapped his arm around her shoulders, saddling up to her. He lowered his voice, making it velvety and smooth.

Her stomach fluttered as his eyes flickering across hers. "You said you didn't want to go to dinner at your parents' alone. I figured I would help you out. It was the least I could do, considering, I was part of the reason you didn't have someone to come with you."

Shaking her head, she covered her face with her hands. "I can't believe this is happening. You don't know my parents. They are meddlers. I'll never hear the end of this." Peeking up from her hands, she studied his face.

"I know." Sean glided his hand down her shoulder, intertwining his fingers with hers. He gave them a slight squeeze. "But... I want you to know that you've changed me. I want to be here with you. I don't plan on messing this up."

"How could you possibly fix this?" She continued through gritted teeth. "You've only made everything harder for me."

Sean considered her words. His eyes danced to hers, melting her to her core. "But I'm trying... I'm trying to make things right."

With no clue on how to respond, she tugged Sean into the dining room.

The dinner went fine. Sean was his charming self. She wished he had some fatal characteristic flaw, anything to keep her from wanting to be with him. The problem was, she couldn't take losing him again or losing everything once more. She wouldn't survive.

Dinner wrapped up, and they all stood to carry the plates to the kitchen sink.

Sean spoke up as they walked into the kitchen. "Melanie, I'm a strong believer that the cook should never have to do the dishes. Why don't you and Noah go relax? Emma and I can clean up."

Melanie smiled. "Great. You won't hear me protest." She set her plate in the sink, patting Emma on the back on the way out. Noah followed behind her into the living room.

Sean and Emma cleaned the dishes in silence, falling into a peaceful routine. Sean washed, then handed dishes to Emma to put into the dishwasher. Soon, he moved onto the pots and pans, scrubbing aggressively with the sponge. In the cupboard, Emma found the kitchen towels for dying and grabbed one.

Sean stopped scrubbing, his hands soapy when he turned to face Emma. "Your parents are really wonderful." His gaze flickered across her face, making her middle warm and knees weak. *Why did he have to look at her that way?*

"Thanks." The word came out shaky. Maybe he knew the spell he casted on her, maybe he didn't, but with trembling hands, she placed the dry platter onto the top shelf of the cupboard, shutting the door. "I know they love me."

"They really do." He spoke softly, like his mind was elsewhere.

Emma's heart skidded to a halt. She had what Sean had never experienced. A cohesive home with two parents who loved her, and each other. His life was still reeling from the devastating effects of his mother abandoning him. The reality hit her.

Sean turned back to the sink, continuing to scrub the pot. "I forgot what it was like..."

Emma leaned up against the counter, inches away from him while he was elbows deep in soapy water. "Forgot what?"

He stopped scrubbing, flipped on the faucet, and rinsed the pot without continuing. Once done, he held the pot out to her. His fingers lingered over hers. Meeting his gaze, she took the pot from him in a daze.

Gripping the edge of the sink with both hands, Sean glanced over at her. Their eyes met, making her temples buzz. She swallowed.

With a strained voice, Sean said, "I forgot what it was like to be a part of a family." The words dangled in the air between them.

Emma stopped drying and considered the agony and longing in his eyes. She saw the little boy waiting for his mom to come home. His heart splintered. Hurt so deep and so wide, it never went away.

Placing the dry pot on the counter, she touched him lightly on the forearm. "I'm sorry you didn't have that growing up. I know I'm lucky. All I've ever wanted is what my parents had because I know it's special. You could have that, Sean. If you gave love a chance."

All the dishes done, Sean turned, leaning his back against the sink. Emma scooted close enough their shoulders were touching. He placed his pinkie finger over hers. The moment serene and intimate, she tried not to panic or worry that the moment would blow through without ever really landing. Instead, she rested her head against his shoulder. Sean wrapped his arm around her. Emma remained silent, waiting for him to respond.

Staring at the windows opposite them, Sean replied, "I can understand now why you want to get married, but you have to understand something..." His voice faded. He stroked the length of her arm. "I'm afraid of all of it. Marriage. Commitment. Loving someone. Afraid that one day I might wake up and the person I chose to love could be gone without a word. I could give into love only to have it reject me in the end. That's why I've run away from it for years. I'm just so scared."

Emma paused. "I understand. Those are all real worries." She wrapped her arm around his waist. "But... What if it did work out? What if you tried, and the woman stayed? What if you loved, and you were loved back? What if you got married and realize you're happier than you ever thought possible?"

Slowly, Sean nodded. "Being here at your home..." Sean squeezed her shoulders. "I want to try."

Emma smiled, tilting her head to him. "Is that right?"

Sean shifted, facing her, he brought her hip to hip. Emma

mirrored his movement, placing her hands flat against his chest. She looked up at him for reassurance. "I'd like to try again with you." Sean cupped her face between his hands. "I'd like to date you with an open mind of marriage being a real option."

Emma sighed, shaking her head. "I don't know." She unlocked her body from his embrace, pushing away from the warmth of his body against hers. She widened the gap, knowing she couldn't trust her emotions with him touching her. "I... This isn't... I've heard this all before." She folded her arms protectively.

"Please." He pleaded. Reaching out for her, he grasped her hand. Their fingers interlocked. "You must believe me. Everything is different with you. Everything that matters."

As much as she wanted to believe him, embrace him, her head screamed all of this would be a waste of time.

Still, with this reasoning, her lips spoke what her head denied but heart embraced. "Okay." She mustered. A word she knew she might regret. Emma bit down on her bottom lip, looking him straight in the eyes. "I'm only giving this thing a few months. I can't waste my time on you if you decide you can't commit."

"That's all the time I need." Sean pulled her near once more.

Her gaze danced to his. "All the time you need for what?"

"To convince you I'm serious this time, to show you in the end I want to be standing next to you forever."

Emma's cheeks flushed. With all her being, she desired his words to be true. He cupped her face. His thumb brushed back and forth along her jawline. She found it hard to concentrate because all she wanted was his lips on hers. "We'll see." Her voice was strained, shaky. "I want that, too."

"I won't screw it up this time." Sean whispered into her

ear. His words dancing across her skin, skimming down her spine. Every part of her was ignited. "I promise."

Slowly, he moved to kiss her tenderly, to gloss over the myriad of feelings from the past. Knees buckling, she fisted his cotton tee in her hand, tugging his body closer. So close, his fiery cologne taunted her, causing her to plunge her tongue into his slightly parted lips. They dipped and dived over hers, traveling to newly discovered places. Finally, breathless, she released her embrace. Sean wrapped his arms around her, giving their hearts a moment to settle.

He lightly kissed her temple, while she snuggled her head against his chest. For a while, they remained in the kitchen. His fingers glided back and forth over the strands of her hair. With every fiber of her being, she yearned for this time to be different. For words to not just be words, but more.

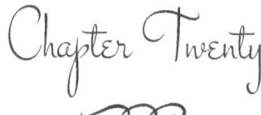

Chapter Twenty

"Emma, just a little longer." Sean slowed down his bike, glancing over at Emma, who was next to him on her bike. "I read there's a nice grassy spot around this bend for us to eat lunch."

Emma smiled. "Great. I'm getting hungry."

Sean pedaled again at a faster pace with Emma alongside him as they followed the trail that hugged the lake. The sunlight shimmered across the water. Up ahead he spotted a nice grassy area to take a break. He slowed down his bike, coming to a halt.

Jumping off, he said, "I think this is a nice place to stop." He walked his bike a few feet and leaned it up against a tree.

Emma followed, and after setting her bike next to his, she pulled out a blanket and picnic from her bicycle basket, spreading the blanket on the grass. The two sat down on it, taking in the view of the lake on a beautiful, warm summer day.

"It's hard to believe this place will be cold come winter." She took her gaze from the lake to her picnic basket and unloaded its contents onto the blanket.

"Thanks for packing all of this." He pulled back the paper, unwrapping his turkey and avocado sandwich and took a bite.

Emma grinned. "Thank the local deli. They packed it all up for me." Emma opened a bag of chips, popping one into her mouth.

"What a nice afternoon." Sean stated contently, in between taking bites of his sandwich.

A voice calling out Emma's name broke the peaceful moment between them. Both turned, peering over their shoulders in the direction of the sound.

A man called out for her again.

"Oh, dear." Emma mumbled under her breath. "What are the odds?"

Breathless, the man stopped right in front of their blanket. "I thought that was you. It's *so* good to see you." He smiled back at her.

Sean's eyes darted between the two of them. Emma brushed off the salt and grease from her hands onto a napkin and stood. Sean followed, joining her.

"Jake... I don't..." Emma stumbled over the words, wringing her hands. "It's been a while."

Protectively, Sean placed his arm around his shoulders. This was the famous Jake? The same one who jilted her at the altar? It had to be. Her glance darted to Sean, wide and wild.

A few beats of time passed. Sean pulled his arm away from her shoulders, extending his hand to him. "I'm Sean. It's nice to meet you."

Jake shook his hand, clearing his throat. "I'm Jake." He waved his hand between him and Emma. "We were engaged at one point."

Emma gnawed on a fingernail. "Yes." She nodded. "True."

Sean scratched his head. "So I've heard..." His blood pressure rose to an astronomical level. He willed himself to remain calm. "Are you here with someone?"

He wanted to push the conversation forward to a point where Jake left, and Emma and he continued their day together undeterred. Though he was unsure of how seeing Jake in person would affect Emma emotionally.

Jake shoved his hands into his pockets. "I came up with an old friend from college. He's taking a quick phone call."

Emma nodded.

Jake's eyes landed squarely on her. "You remember Tyson, right?"

She inhaled. "I do," replied Emma.

"Sorry... This is such a surprise." Jake's stare moved to Sean. "Do you mind if I speak with Emma privately for a moment?"

Sean cleared his throat, his fists tightening. "I believe that's up to Emma." His eyes narrowed at the man who broke Emma's heart. The one who no doubt now realized the error of his ways and planned to get her back.

Emma glanced over at Sean, and squeezed his hand. "I'm okay... Give me a minute to talk to Jake, and I'll right back."

Sean tried his best to smile, while inside he was spiraling. He caressed her hand with his thumb as she squeezed it once more. "No problem. I'll wait here."

His heart began to pick up speed, while his hands became clammy. He wondered if this was how he would lose her. It was written all over Jake's face. The man had a face full of remorse. Why else did he need to speak with her alone?

Emma blinked, nodding. "Thanks." She let go of his hand and swung her glance back at Jake. "Let's walk up this path for a minute and chat."

The two walked off. Settling back onto the blanket, Sean stared at them as they continued down the path until they were out of his sight. His hands shaky, stomach churning, he forced himself to take a swig of his soda. The carbonation bubbled down his throat, dampening the burning acid coating his middle. Over the last several months, Emma had become completely embedded in his heart.

Bored, he munched on some chips as he tried to pass the time. He made himself think of anything but losing Emma. He couldn't lose her, not now, not when she was all that mattered. There was only one woman in the world who he would marry, and that was Emma. *Whoa, where did that come from?* He waited for the nerves to set in from his revelation, but it didn't. Resolved, if she came back and chose him, he would marry her. No more excuses.

Moments ticked by. Sean laid back on the blanket, cradling his head with his hands. The sky was a brilliant blue, just like it was on the day he met Emma. Sean closed his eyes, letting himself bathe in the warmth of its rays. Inhaling, he forced his heart and mind to settle. Emma was a smart woman. She would choose wisely and by wisely, he believed it was him. Then he drifted off.

Sometime later there was some crumbling on the blanket that woke him. He shot straight up, stretching. His eyes adjusted. "Everything okay?" His gaze fluttered across her face.

Kneeling back down on the blanket, Emma sighed. "I think so."

She met his eyes and held his gaze for several seconds. All he could hear was the pounding of his heart. He longed to hear she was still his. He glanced down at his watch. Emma had been gone for over an hour. His stomach plummeted.

Fiddling around, he took a sip of his soda. Anything to calm his nerves and help him calm down before he spoke. It was imperative he didn't mess this whole thing up by jumping to conclusions or not allowing her the time and space to explain what had happened. "Was it a good conversation? Did it help you find closure?"

Emma rubbed her hands back and forth on top of her

shorts. She glanced out at the lake and not at him. "He apologized." She finally brought her gaze back to him.

Desperately, he wondered what had transpired. If things between them had shifted. He forced himself to speak slowly and calmly. "Okay... And was that helpful?"

"I think it was." Emma reached out and took his hand. Her skin was warm and inviting. It grounded him back to the world where it was him and Emma.

He let his thumb glide over the top of her hand, a constant circular motion. With his free hand, Sean rubbed the back of his neck, searching for the words, ones which would bring them closer together instead of creating a divide. "I'm glad it was helpful. Anything else happen that you don't mind sharing?" *There, that sounded rational.*

Emma scooted closer to him on the blanket, he wrapped his arm around her shoulders. She leaned against him, her finger tracing a line back and forth over the top of his thigh. It left a blazing trail of heat. He willed himself to remain steady.

She glanced up at him, her hand settling on his chest. "Like I told you, he apologized... Then he asked if we could try again."

Sean sucked in a deep breath. This couldn't be happening. His worst nightmare was coming true. Falling for a woman, finally ready to pledge his life to her, then in one fell swoop, it was gone. *Whoa, back up. Calm down. Listen.*

"Is..." His voice was shaky, revealing what he had no ability to hide. "Is that what you want?" The world became quite as he anticipated her reply. All he heard was his heart in his temples.

Emma gazed at him. "No." She moistened her lips, pulling him closer. "I told him he was too late. My heart belonged with someone else... With you."

Sean grinned. His middle a warm gooey mess. The words he longed to hear, washing over him, and carrying away the moment of doubt. Reaching forward, he tucked a few loose strands of hair behind her ear. Then he cupped her face with his hand. "You make me so happy, and my heart belongs to you, too. I plan on marrying you someday."

Emma smirked. "Really?"

"I mean it." He stated firmly, without reservation. "I'm going to marry you."

Her fingers skidded across the collar of his shirt, searing his skin wherever it cared to travel. "You seem awful confident." Emma's eyes sparkled back at him. "What makes you think I'll say yes?"

He shrugged, smiling. "A feeling."

Emma raised an eyebrow. "A feeling?" She laughed.

"Yes." He confirmed, his gaze locking with hers. He tried to remember a time when she wasn't in his life, a time when he didn't love her.

Every part of him ached to kiss her. Without reservation, he crossed the few inches of space between them, letting his lips slide over hers. Time stopped. The world around him faded. All the worries and hurts of the past were gone. He pulled her closer, allowing himself to discover her more fully, making his lips dance across hers. She tightened her grip, melting into his arms. He breathed in her luscious scent, memorizing the silky feel of her hair between his fingers. Learning by heart the outline of her jaw, while his finger traveled the smooth surface of her skin. Reluctantly, breathless, he forced himself to pull away.

Bringing her face between both of his hands, foreheads touching, he waited for the thumping of his heart to return to its steady pace. "I love you," he whispered. The words permeating the very air they breathed.

Her eyes locked with his own, holding him steady and keeping him captive. Sean was no longer afraid of the future.

Emma kissed him lightly on the cheek. "I love you, too."

He was healed and whole with her in his arms. "And you..." Sean kissed her lightly on the temple. "Emma... you're the only one I've ever really loved."

Emma smiled, gripping a fist full of his cotton tee. She tugged him close, her lips a mere inch from his own. "You... you're my everything." Then she leaned in and kissed him.

Epilogue

Sean flipped off his office light, wandering back to the waiting room of his clinic. With the long days of summer still with them, the sun began its descent. Families walked by the big windows, laughing and talking with one another.

His phone rang, breaking his happy trance. He reached back into his pocket, glancing at the screen.

Smiling, he brought the phone to ear and answered, "Dad."

Sean placed his phone in the crook of his neck as he made once last sweep of his clinic before locking up.

"How's everything going with you? I know it's been a while since we've talked." His dad's voice was upbeat.

The marriage Sean thought was a sham, had turned out to be the exact opposite. Thomas had never been happier.

"I'm doing fine." Sean flicked off the lobby light. "How's Lisa?" He was trying because he finally understood the beauty of being in love.

Thomas hesitated for a beat, but then answered with extra enthusiasm. "Great. Thanks so much for asking. We finished a big sweep of visiting all her kids. We wanted to head back up toward you next week. Would that work? Will you be around?"

Sean dug around in his bag, locating his keys. "I'll be around. I'd love to see..." He almost said you but thought better of it. "I'd love to see you and Lisa. Please come."

"I look forward to it."

"Me, too." Sean closed the door, locking it. "Dad..." He walked to the bottom of his stairs leading up to his apartment, pausing. "I've met someone." There, he said it. He divulged what he had failed to mention before out of fear. "She's terrific. I think you'll really like her. I'd like to introduce you and Lisa to her when you're in town." He fiddled with his keys, worried about broaching the next subject he wanted to address.

"I...I'd be honored," responded Thomas.

"Dad?"

"What is it, Sean?" asked Thomas.

"I'm going to marry this one," revealed Sean. Thomas was silent.

Sean pulled the phone away from his ear, glancing down at his phone screen. Checking the connection, he placed the phone back to his ear. "You still there?"

"I'm here." Thomas paused, his voice cracking. "I never thought I would hear those words."

Sean laughed, lightening the mood. "I never thought I would say them."

Thomas finally laughed, too. "Look at us, son. Two guys who finally found a way to love again."

"I know." Sean smiled to himself. "I never would've believed it was possible, but Emma's different. She accepts all of me, even the broken and fragile parts."

Thomas cleared his throat. "That's how I feel about Lisa."

Sean smiled again. Gratitude seeped into his heart, thinking of the two of them moving past the rocky abandonment of his mom and onto a more solid footing. "I'm happy Lisa has brought joy into your life. You deserve every bit of it."

"Thanks, Sean. It's means the world to me that you accept Lisa."

Sean finally entered his apartment, closing the door behind him. He dropped his belongings inside, then strode across the room, settling onto his couch.

"One more thing…" Sean hesitated. The words were hard to say. The question pressing on his mind. He exhaled. "Do you think I will make a good husband? Dad?"

"The best." Thomas added, so quickly that it startled Sean.

"Really?" Sean shifted in his seat, anxious and unsure of himself, desiring some reassurance that he was capable of what he wanted with Emma. "How can you know?"

"Because… I raised you. I know you are a good man. Despite our broken home, you managed to become a wonderful person," stated Thomas. "You've changed a lot since I first introduced you to Lisa. I know now that had to do with this woman in your life, but if she is the one you want to marry, then do it. Don't punish yourself any longer. Give in to happiness."

Sean let Thomas' words penetrate his heart, giving it the needed healing balm. "Thanks, dad. I owe it all to you. I don't think you have any idea how much you mean to me."

Thomas paused. "Yes, I do…" His voice cracked. "Because you mean just as much to me. If not more… I love you, son."

"I love you, dad." Sean smiled. His dad was a man of few words, so this conversation meant more to him than Thomas could ever know.

"See you next week." Thomas added.

Sean grinned. "I can't wait."

* * *

The summer months passed. Fall became a blur. The colors of fall gave way to winter. Snow covered the ground. Emma approached a year since that pivotal day on the ski slopes. A trip which ended far better than it started. Sean was the unanticipated prize, the one to draw her out and save her from a dark and dreary time.

Emma and Sean walked through downtown Bluebird holding hands. The shops had placed their holiday decorations in the windows, and the two admired the displays. Peering into the shop window, she pointed at the beautiful window display showing a wide array of Christmas ornaments.

She tugged on Sean's hand, pulling him closer. "Look at these beautiful ornaments." Taking a step closer to the window, she scanned the intricately painted bulbs. "I can't believe someone painted those... And that Christmas is around the corner." She glanced over her shoulder at him, catching his eye.

Sean smiled. His blue ocean eyes sparkling back at her. "Neither can I." He gave her gloved hand a squeeze. The gesture still managed to melt her middle.

The two began walking once more along the street while the lampposts lighted their way. Emma was on winter break from teaching, and the two had plans to split the time between Christmas with her family and Sean's for New Year's. After Christmas, they were driving north to meet Thomas and Lisa at one of Sean's new stepsiblings' houses. A first even for him.

Emma looped her hands around the crook of Sean's elbow, leaning against him. "It was nice meeting Lisa and Thomas a few months ago." She reflected on the happy meeting.

"What was that?" asked Sean, distracted. He pulled his gaze from the sidewalk in front of them, and back to Emma.

"It was nice meeting Lisa and Thomas. They seem happy

together." She smiled. "Are you nervous about meeting all of your stepsiblings?"

"Let me just say, I'm glad you'll be there with me." Sean patted the top of her hand. "I don't know if I could do it on my own, but with you there beside me, I'm sure it will go fine."

Arriving at the restaurant, the same one they ate at for the first time together, Sean opened the door, holding it while she stepped inside.

The restaurant was warm and cozy. Emma stripped off her coat and gloves. Smiling, she reached out and wrapped her arm around his waist. He wrapped his arm around her shoulders. "I'm glad I can go with you to meet them. Don't worry, I'll be there with you every part of the way."

Sean squeezed her shoulders. "I know you will."

The host led them to their booth. The one which faced the front windows, overlooking Main Street. Both settled into their seats and took the menus from the host. The fire roaring next to them made Emma's cheeks warm, and she pushed up the sleeves of her shirt. After deciding what she wanted, she folded back up the menu and placed it on the table.

"You decide what you want?" Sean asked while his eyes scanned the selections.

"Yep." Emma brought her elbow up on the table, cradling her chin under her hand. She glanced out the window. "You think it might snow tonight?"

Sean peeled his eyes away from the menu, closing it. Then he reached for her hand. "What did you say?"

Emma pulled her attention from the window back to Sean. He was acting aloof and out of it. She wondered if he had a stressful day at work, or if he was nervous about the upcoming holidays and all that it involved. "Hey, is everything okay with you?" She squeezed his hand. "You seem distracted."

EMI HILTON

"What?" Sean shifted in his seat. His eyes flickering back and forth and all around, anywhere but at her.

She continued searching his face. "Everything okay? You seem..." She shook her head, then waved her free hand. "Forget it... It just seems like something is off with you tonight."

"Really?" Sean let go of her hand, nervously tugging at his shirt collar.

"Yes." Emma studied him.

Should she be worried? The last several months were a whirlwind. Each day better than the one before. The love she had for Sean was far deeper and richer than anything she ever experienced with Jake. The two held no comparison. Sean had her heart. If, for some unforeseeable reason they didn't end up together, Emma knew there would never be another for her. He was the one. The man she placed all her chips on.

In the beginning, several months back, Sean had his moments of anxiety with commitment. He had to work through the issues of his childhood and the feelings of abandonment with his misconceived notion of being unlovable. Sean grew in his capacity to accept and give love. The entire process had bonded them together in ways she never imagined possible. Out of everyone in the world, Emma only wanted him.

Sean nervously laughed. "How do you know me so well?"

Emma smiled. "I just do, so, out with it. What's going on?" She eyed him suspiciously.

He slid out of the booth, standing in front of her. "I'm nervous, because I'm going to do this." Kneeling, he pulled out a ring box from his pocket and flipped open the case.

Emma gasped, tears immediately stinging the corners of her eyes. Her hands covered her mouth. "Sean." Her voice was soft and tender. She tilted her head to the side.

"I love you so much, Emma. More than I ever thought possible. You have stood by me, guiding me to a place of love and acceptance. I can't imagine a life where you aren't in it, next to me. Please marry me."

The restaurant became quiet.

Emma stared at Sean. "Of course, I'll marry you!" She leaped from her seat, embracing him. The restaurant erupted in applause and cheers.

Sean slid the sparkly diamond ring onto her finger while she wiped her tears. Leaning forward, her lips grazed his. They parted, and she tasted the minty flavor of his mouth. His spicy cologne whirled between them, making her head spin. A swooning sensation filled her stomach. Pulling away, she smiled up at him. Their eyes met.

"I love you." She whispered.

Sean leaned in close, whispering into her ear. "I love you, too." His words tickled her neck, cascading down her back. He kissed her on the temple. The people in the restaurant still cheering, he shouted out to the crowd. "I'm getting married!"

Emma laughed in delight, knowing all the heartbreak of the past was long gone. It catapulted her forward, right to where she belonged with Sean, in Bluebird, with him holding her.

Acknowledgments

I am indebted to my readers. Thank you for following me on my writing journey. For purchasing my books, sharing with a friend, and leaving five-star reviews. You are helping me live out my dream.

To my beta readers, Carolyn Williams, Elise Thomas, Kaylin Padgett and Sara Ostler. Thank you for your thoughtful feedback. For taking the time to read Sean and Emma's love story in its most raw form. You helped to direct the story in the direction it was always meant to go.

To my editor, thank you for your patience with me. For working with me to improve my writing. This love story became polished through your steady eye.

To my publisher Parcel and Page, it's been one of the greatest honors of my life to work with you. My deepest appreciation to you for taking a chance on a newbie writer like me. I will forever be in your debt.

To my husband, my constant and faithful companion, I love you more than anything. Thank you for giving me my own happily-ever-after.

To my parents, siblings, extended family, and friends. Each of you sprinkle my life with color and variety. Your love and encouragement catapult me forward when I stumble. I appreciate every one of you in different and unique ways. Though I can't thank you all individually, you know who you are, and I am thankful for all the ways in which our paths are connected.

Last, I thank God, my faithful Father in Heaven. I know

all things are possible with thee. I praise thy name and devote all the glory and honor to thee. May all know of thy unending goodness, grace, and mercy.

About the Author

Emi Hilton is a California native who was born at March Airforce Base, while her father was an Officer in the US Army Combat Engineer Battalion.

An English Professor for a mother, Emi followed in her mother's footsteps and graduated from Brigham Young University in English. While in college, she took a year and a half break from her studies to serve as a full-time missionary for her church in the Canary Islands.

When Emi isn't writing, she enjoys training for marathons, fishing off local piers with her husband and three sons, or visiting her other love, Spain.

Also by Emi Hilton

Memories in Morro Bay